The Deepwater Trilogy

Deepwater Black
Deepwater Landing
Deepwater Angels

Deepwater Landing

Ken Catran

Hodder
Children's
Books

a division of Hodder Headline plc

First published in New Zealand 1993
by HarperCollins Publishers New Zealand Ltd.

First published in Great Britain in 1995
by Hodder Children's Books

10 9 8 7 6 5 4 3 2 1

A Catalogue record for this book is available from the British Library

ISBN 0 340 62673 9

Typeset by Avon Dataset Ltd, Bidford-on-Avon, B50 4JH

Printed and bound in Great Britain by
Cox & Wyman Ltd, Reading, Berks

Hodder Children's Books
A Division of Hodder Headline plc
338 Euston Road
London NW1 3BH

For Wendy

Contents

	Prologue	1
1	The space-side of me	3
2	Life forms	7
3	Aliens like us	15
4	Space fight	23
5	Blackout	31
6	Unseen enemy	39
7	The enemy takes shape	47
8	More trouble	55
9	Ambush in Colour-space	63
10	Battle inside Deepwater	71
11	The creature from NUN	81
12	Hide and seek with something evil	89
13	The electronic vampire strikes	99
14	Ghost lights	107
15	Monster from the death ship	117
16	Deepwater sun storm	125
17	Reeboks springs a trap	131
18	The power rings of COL	139
19	Aliens in the darkness	149
20	Time-busters	159
21	The last enemy	167
22	Death ride of a gene ark	175

Prologue

Deepwater is the name of a spaceship. It is flying about half a million years in the future, far beyond the known universe. It was built to penetrate the final unknown of 'Colour-space', that strange, galactic jungle of alien life-forms that exists just before the end of time itself.

There are six crew on Deepwater. They are all teenagers and their commander is a girl with blonde and red hair, called Yoona. They have no other life but the spaceship, because Deepwater took off from a solar colony on Mars in the year 2090, long before they were born.

Deepwater was built to cross the entire universe, so its crew is very special. An ordinary crew could not survive the impossible distances by any known means of space travel. This crew was cloned from gene cells on the spaceship and grew up under the care of a super bio-computer called NUN.

But something had gone wrong. After all those many thousands of years crossing the universe, NUN became too possessive. It did not teach the children everything about their spaceship – which meant they had to find out by themselves. And because they were cloned from gene cells they have another problem. Every gene has a built-in slice of memory and they can live with this memory, like a time-trip. This is 'pre-existing', which they call 'prexing'. With their hi-tech brain-scanners they can enter each other's 'prexes' and live that part of the past life.

So the teenagers of Deepwater live two lives: their real

lives on the spaceship and part of a past life. The past life is like one episode of a serial.

They live on Deepwater and they live their past life. They are fighting against a known past and an unknown future. In the first book, the Earth-boy Robbie Mikkelson found himself in the body of the teenage crew member, Reb. In his struggle for identity, he had the help of another Earthkid, Denie Miles.

There are eight crew-persons on Deepwater. But only six have woken in their crystal caskets. Denie Miles will find she is the seventh. And *Deepwater Landing* is her book.

1 The space-side of me

A spaceship thousands of years into the unknown . . . alien creatures and the survival of human life in the universe. It all happened the night that Mum, Dad and I played Scrabble. Dad cooked dinner and I was thinking about what Robbie Mikkelson had told me about Deepwater and its mission across the universe.

Mum won the Scrabble. She crowed for five seconds, then noticed I was looking pale. She asked if there was something wrong and I said there wasn't. I was still looking for rational explanations then and had almost decided Robbie got his signals crossed over some bad dreams. Then the first bad thing happened.

When getting ready for bed, I felt a strange crawly feeling up and down my body; just for a second, as though I was in a different blackness, breathing different air. Where was my duvet? The bed felt hard and padded. Then my hand hit something as I reached up and my elbows banged into sides. I was trapped in a box and I screamed to wake up out of the nightmare. Then the solid roof seemed to lift and I saw light and shadows overhead.

I sat up. This was all one of those super-real strange dreams, it had to be. Ahead of me was a row of what looked unpleasantly like coffins. They were made of some glassy substance that twinkled in the half-light. And all around, the huge room stretched into shadows that made it even bigger. Crystal coffins in a huge room. Oh, this had to be a dream because the reality was too impossible even to think about. Then from the shadows came that terrible hating presence, as though something evil was closing invisible monster claws round me.

I turned and ran, ran as fast as I could across that empty room that stretched on before me in the shadows. The floor was metal; my footsteps echoed round me and that evil unseen thing was swooping down on me. Something ice-cold tingled round my body like a hand grabbing me, then I was through a door and running down a long corridor. Lights were coming on ahead of me, shutting off behind, and the strong sense of evil somehow fell behind.

Then I was through another door, in another room. This one had black metal bunks, and from across the room a strange figure with staring eyes looked at me. She had a brown-red face and red hair and wore a silver-grey track suit. I pointed at her and opened my mouth to say something – she did the same. I was looking in a mirror!

The sense of evil had gone but the nightmare was crowding round. I think I knew even then what all this was, but I was still in shock. There were metal stairs ahead and I ran up them into that place of my dream – the metal chairs, the rows of consoles and the eye-shaped windows. But it was different this time because instead of black, they showed a blue-yellow sky. And before the consoles stood a girl, dressed in the same silver-grey track suit as me. She had long blonde and red hair and she turned as I came up the stairs and gaped at me. I knew where I was and I knew who she was, but I still had to ask.

'Where I am?'

'On Deepwater,' she said.

She was saying something else, I think trying to reassure me. But everything went black for a moment and when I opened my eyes, she was standing over me, splashing some water on my face, patting my cheeks. She looked really uptight about something, but tried to give me a big reassuring grin.

4

'It's all right, you're all right, Cei, you're among friends.'

Cei? Yes, the name was black-lettered on my track suit. Just as hers was; Yoona. I was on the spaceship, unless this was a super-real dream because of everything Robbie had said . . .

'Robbie . . .' I managed to whisper.

Yoona's hand went tight on my arm. 'Cei, how do you know about Reb?'

'Denie Miles . . .' My tongue felt like it was stuck to my mouth with glue. 'My name is Denie Miles. I'm a school-friend of Robbie's . . .'

'You're another Earth-gene,' she whispered, 'from one of the closed caskets . . .' She looked at me, then pulled at her long hair and shook her head like she didn't believe anything. 'COL!' she suddenly shouted.

COL, their voice-activated computer. 'What's the matter?' I said weakly.

'COL isn't responding,' she said. 'I woke out of deep sleep like you half an hour ago, and came up here.' She looked around, *really* uptight now. 'Nothing makes sense.'

And it was then I realised something else – sunshine on those metal steps and blue-yellow sky through the eye-windows. 'Are we back on Earth?' I whispered. Had Deepwater completed its mission?

But even before Yoona shook her head, I knew I was wrong. The sun in this sky was blue-yellow, larger and closer. When I stood up on my wobbly legs I could see clumps of dark green-blue trees and patches of yellow grass. The whole thing looked as though it had been filtered through crazy-coloured glass. It seemed like the trees were just below the window.

No wonder Yoona was in shock. There is only one known solar system in the universe – a sun complete with revolving planets – and that is Earth's; our own. This sun was too different and that meant we were somewhere unknown.

Deepwater had landed on an alien planet.

5

2   Life forms

'COL, report status!' Yoona shouted again.

Nothing. COL – Control Operational Link, our voice-activated guidance computer – was silent. And Yoona should have freaked out by now, but she just took a deep breath and snapped herself back on-line. I could see why she was in command.

'I have to sort this out first,' she said, meaning my Cei/Denie problem would have to wait. 'Something has stopped Deepwater and COL's not answering.' She was going downstairs, talking on the run. I took a last fascinated look at the blue-yellow sky and followed. Below deck, Yoona unclipped a metal locker from the end of her bunk and opened it, then did the same with another.

'Do you feel well enough to help?' She gave me a tense look.

'Sure. But shouldn't we wait for the others?'

Yoona just shook her head. She'd pulled out two space suits and was scrambling into hers, shouting for COL as she did. There was still no answer. I tried to put mine on; it was like heavy overalls, and Yoona helped me. Her face was pale.

'I'll do a circuit of the ship, see if anything's holding us down.'

'Do you want me to come too?' It was awesome even to think about, but Yoona shook her head again.

'Just operate the exit port.'

She strapped on her heavy, magnetic shoes and knelt

to put mine on. Then the helmets, and we clanged over to the port airlock. It hissed open and we clanged through. I knew that Yoona and Robbie had escaped down these airlocks once from the jel monster that NUN had sent against them. The glass over the control button was still broken.

The second airlock hissed open and my breath misted the helmet visor. Yoona knew I was scared; she touched my arm and gave a little smile as the third door opened. But I could feel a crazy surge of excitement, too. This was unreal and it was happening! Then the last airlock shut behind us and we were in the exit chamber.

Blue-yellow light shone through the heavy iron-glass of the big exit port. Both side walls had a pair of small, round metal doors set in them. Yoona pressed a button over one and a little metal craft pushed out. It had pincer arms and a glass canopy with two bulging eyes. An OMA, Robbie had called it – Outside Maintenance Auxiliary.

Yoona sealed my helmet, then hers. Her voice came on the intercom as she opened the canopy. 'I'll be as quick as I can. Stand by to open the port.'

'You'd better show me how to use that thing. I may have to come after you.'

Yoona hesitated, then nodded. 'OK.' She gave me a hurried run-over of the OMA controls. They were simple, like a kiddy-car. 'I hope you don't have to.'

'So do I.'

'We don't know what this planet is like.' She was scrambling into the OMA. 'And without COL . . .'

She stopped. I already knew quite a lot about COL from Robbie. It was voice-activated to Yoona and when she spoke COL's name, there was a tiny ringing echo like a tuning-fork. She stood up in the OMA.

'COL, report status!'

'Stationary orbit, planet four, solar system—' then followed a string of a billion-billion light-year numbers. The voice was deep, not male or female, sounding like the cool shadows of an old church.

Yoona was still angry. 'COL, why haven't you been responding?'

'This is the first time you have spoken.'

'No, it's—' She broke off. There was no point standing here arguing. 'Come on, Cei.'

She was getting out of the OMA. Even in the space suit and metal shoes she could move! We nearly ran back through the airlock doors to the lower deck and began taking off the suits. Yoona kept talking, as though afraid COL would go away again.

'COL, why are we in stationary orbit?'

'Programme order,' came the super-cool voice.

'COL, we gave you no programme order to stop here.'

'Programme order is from the first mission.'

Yoona gritted her teeth. 'Like talking to a kid sometimes,' she muttered to me, then drew a deep breath. 'COL – *what* programme order?'

'Recharging.'

Recharging what? We took off the rest of our gear and went back up to the main deck. Yoona collapsed in her chair and began rapid-fire questions to COL.

Deepwater was (said COL) a solar-charged spaceship, but still had to make things like food and water. The position of this solar system was known by the twenty-first century (when Deepwater was launched) and was a refuelling link. It had a planet whose atmosphere was suitable to restock on all the nutrients needed for the next interstellar lap of our journey.

As simple as that. 'Makes sense,' I said. 'Most long trips need at least one gas stop.'

Yoona sat up. 'But why wake us – and not the others?' She spoke over the console. 'COL, why were we woken up?'

'No instructions.'

'COL, did *you* wake us up?'

9

'No.'

'You're sure?'

'Yes.'

Yoona was still worried. She began scanning course readings on her console. I looked out of the long observation windows. The spaceship had not quite landed, but was hovering just over a big clump of trees below. They were rounded and green-blue, with bright red fruit like huge apples. Yoona spoke again.

'Cei, I'm going to scan the memory banks. It'll take time. Have a look round and don't touch anything.'

'Yoona, please call me Denie.' I just got an absent nod back; Yoona's mind was on the console. 'Hey, COL glitched. What's the problem?'

'COL isn't supposed to glitch.'

'Can I – can I go as far as the exit port and look out?'

'No!' Yoona gave me an uptight look. 'We can't take the chance of opening Deepwater to an alien atmosphere.'

'I'll keep the airlock doors shut, Yoona. Please, I want to be a science journalist . . .'

She interrupted. 'Denie, your prex world stopped existing thousands of years ago.'

I resented the way she said that. I should have realised how concerned she was about COL. But part of me was still in shock, too. 'All right then, I promise not to touch anything!'

'Denie . . .'

My turn to cut her off. I was already heading for the stairs and didn't stop. I felt like a kid being sent out of class. I went below and sat down. Then I started feeling really angry with myself for reacting like that. I'd forgotten all my own lessons on self-control. I counted backwards from ten, then took a few deep breaths and felt better.

Then a little wriggle of panic started in my stomach. Yoona was right. Everything I knew was gone and I was on Deepwater. I was sitting in a spaceship and outside was an alien planet. I had to go back on deck, tell Yoona I was sorry for being stupid – and see as much as I could from the windows. I stood up and the deck hatch slid shut.

Was that Yoona's way of making sure I didn't get into trouble? Lock me in, down here? How could Robbie like that cold and bossy young woman? Then a voice crackled on the intercom, heavy with static.

'Denie, take out an OMA. Check the hull for entry damage.'

I jumped up. 'Me? Are you sure?'

The static cleared. It was Yoona's voice all right, sounding impatient. 'Yes, I'm sure. Do it.' The first airlock door slid open.

She'd changed her mind! I just threw myself back into the space suit, clicked on the helmet, snapped the visor shut and clanged into the first airlock. It closed and the second opened. Then the third. I was still scared, but riding high. Yoona was in command of Deepwater and she had told me to go, so it must be OK. The fourth airlock slid open and I was in the exit port again.

And there was the bright, shiny little six-legged OMA, out of its tunnel like a crayfish from its hole. The airlock door slid shut behind me. Oh, Yoona was wonderful – she trusted me and I wouldn't let her down.

'Do you remember how to handle the OMA, Denie?' Even her voice was soft and sweet now.

'Yes.'

She went through it again anyway, while I got into the OMA. A control stick for direction, foot-pedals for stopping and starting, sensor-gloves to operate the long pincer arms.

'Ready, Denie?' Soft and sweet? Yoona had a beautiful voice, but it was so strong it vibrated in my helmet intercom. Then the big exit port cartwheeled sideways. Outside was a circle of blue-yellow sky and just at the bottom of the port, one of those green-blue trees with red fruit.

'Go, Denie!'

11

I felt like Columbus, Cook and Marco Polo rolled into a great Female One. I moved the stick forward, the metal legs tucked up neatly and the OMA glided out with a tiny humming noise.

It was suddenly a bit scary to have empty space underneath, but I'd done a little hang-gliding with Dad and soon got used to it. I turned the OMA round in a wide circle.

'No sign of hull damage so far.'

Yoona didn't answer at once but I didn't care, it was all too wonderful. I'd never realised how big and long Deepwater was. You have to think of one of those mirror-glass block skyscrapers lying on its side, shaped a little like a giant whale. Big side-vents were opening and closing like gills on a fish as Deepwater basked in the blue-yellow sunlight.

Yoona had talked about doing a circuit underneath, so I took the OMA along the side and down, like a tiny water-beetle under the belly of this cosmic whale. The blue-yellow sky was overhead, with a broad distant band of white across it. Below was a forest of the tall green-blue trees, more than I remembered from the first time we saw them. They were hundreds of metres high and topped with clusters of those big red fruit.

I circled the OMA and the branches almost seemed to wave at me. I nearly shouted with delight. This was an alien planet in an alien solar system and I was the very first to see all this! Above me, Deepwater hovered, the silver-glass plates flashing a blue-yellow in the sunlight.

'Check under the spaceship – and those trees.' Yoona's voice was so warm and friendly now. Maybe she'd found out there was nothing wrong with COL.

'OK, Yoona.'

I took the OMA down between the arches of those incredible giant trees and could not resist flying through. They closed overhead like a beautiful green-blue cathedral roof. One of the red fruit fell past the window and splattered

12

itself on the ground, bursting in a cloud of sticky red powder.

Magic . . . oh, so beautiful and unbelievable. One Earth-hour ago, I was lying in my bed and now I was flying through a strange and lovely alien forest. There was no sign of life, just those rows of wonderful huge trees with glossy, dark green trunks that seemed to go on forever. I'd nearly forgotten Yoona.

I turned the OMA round and it nearly brushed against the side of the trees. They were closer than they looked. Then I turned down the way I'd come and another red fruit came sailing down and exploded on the ground. The powder seemed to rise like a dark red mist and suddenly I was worried. The trees should have broken now into the open patch where I came through. But they were closed in a green-blue leafy tunnel.

'Yoona,' I said. There was no answer. I felt an unpleasant thrill of something going wrong and twisted the stick, spinning the OMA round. I gasped in horror.

'Yoona!'

Behind, the tunnel had also slid shut at the other end, like a blue-green door. As it did, more of the red globes fell and exploded, and the air was blinded with red dust.

I choked with panic and spun the OMA round as the horrible mass seemed to close in on me like the jaws of an insect-eating plant.

'Yoona!' Still no answer.

I jerked the control stick back and the OMA shot up. There were still hints of blue-yellow sky but the branches were interlocking and threw me back. It was like bouncing against a trampoline. More of the red fruit fell and the powder rose in a thick scarlet cloud. I jerked the control stick again and slipped my hand into the sensor-glove, making a frantic cutting movement as I shot back up. Would it work the claw?

We crashed against the leaf-mass and it recoiled as though hurt. Yes! The OMA burst through, bits of green-blue

13

scattering everywhere. In the same moment, there was an angry shout in my intercom.

'Denie!'

Above me, Deepwater was moving, the observation eyes seemed to glare down. Then a green-blue branch-hand swung and threw a handful of the red globes at the OMA. They covered the glass thickly just as another green-blue something wrapped round the OMA's tail. The red powder was blotting everything out. The OMA jerked and we spun crazily. Yoona was shouting something, but it was lost in the mad blackness that jerked me flat on something bouncy, my legs entangled.

I tried to kick myself free, yelling. Then the light went on and Mum was in the bedroom, looking at me.

3   Aliens like us

'Denie, are you all right?'

It was just after dawn and I could hear rain against the windows. I blinked, so dazed by the sudden sharp change that I couldn't speak. Mum sat down on the side of the bed.

'You gave an awful yell – what's wrong?' That was Dad in his terrible yellow pyjamas, hair in the usual mess.

I've had a prex and it was horrible, that's what's wrong. But I can't talk to you about it, Mum and Dad. That's what I should have said. My duvet was still tangled round my legs and I shook my head.

'I'm OK. I just had a bad dream.'

'You never have bad dreams.' Dad nudged Mum and she took the hint. 'OK, lollipop, call us if you have another.' They left.

Lollipop. She must have been concerned because they *know* I don't like that nickname – I even stopped wearing striped tops because of it. I sat there while the rain grew heavier and my head did a sick, slow spin. I was almost afraid to close my eyes in case I opened them again in that terrible living forest. And right now I wasn't sure who I was and where exactly I should be. Was this really a prex cycle, or my super-active imagination?

Dad was out on an early call. The rain made it too wet for bikes, so Mum drove me to school. She asked a little too casually about the bad dream, but I just started talking about how rain would mean no hockey. And all the time I was thinking about Deepwater, about Yoona letting me outside

15

– then sounding angry when she saw me again. There were just too many questions.

Mum stopped by the school. 'Look after yourself, Loll—' She stopped hastily as she saw my look, gave me a quick kiss and drove off. I heard a lip-smacking sound behind me and turned. It was Reeboks, leaning on the handlebars of his bike. He had on so much wet-weather gear he looked like a frog.

'Nice kiss from Mummy, little, wee, baby girlie?' he jeered.

I only meant to brush past him, but he must have been off balance. His bike went over with a crash and Reeboks ended up in a puddle. He wasn't hurt but got up, yelling madly.

'You did that on purpose. Me and Meatgrinder will get you for that!'

'It was an accident, pencil-neck,' came a voice behind me. Robbie Mikkelson. Reeboks just snarled and went off. 'Don't turn your back on the little rat,' said Robbie.

'Thanks.' He was right. Reeboks was sidekick and evil genius to Meatgrinder, the school bully and a real thicko. They were running a little protection racket and our teacher, Ms Booth, busted it up. Reeboks thinks I told her. I didn't, but he needed someone to blame. And it was unreal talking to Robbie because there was another Robbie – on Deepwater.

'Can I borrow your bike at lunch-time?' I said. There was something I had to do. He looked at me, puzzled and with the words 'No way' forming on his lips. Then I think a little part of his space-side memory clicked and he nodded.

Meatgrinder flicked pellets at me all through morning class. Ms Booth, who normally has eyes in the back of her head, didn't see him. I couldn't wait to get to the bike sheds and whizzed down the school drive, accidentally spraying a puddle over Ms Booth. She shouted something, but I kept going. This was really becoming my day.

It was twenty minutes' fast biking to the lab. This year

16

we'd done a school project on biology and genes. Well, Robbie's gene had ended up on that spaceship and so had mine. And the woman giving the lecture had taken some hair and little specks of blood from us to show how easy it was to take a gene sample.

I was in the door, past the receptionist and down the corridor before I slowed. I didn't know what to say, or if I should be here. I couldn't talk about Yoona and Deepwater because it was sounding like a crazy dream now, even to me. The lab door was ahead and the name-plate read 'Chibbi Orduna'. I pushed it open and went in.

A woman in a white coat was sitting with her back to me. I didn't know what to say and suddenly I became scared. And being scared made me shout the first thing that came into my mind.

'Did you take my gene and keep it?'

Ms Orduna must have been having her lunch. She jumped up and turned round, coughing and waving her plastic fork around. She swallowed and managed to speak.

'I took your *what*?'

I hadn't meant to say it that way. I tried to tell her, but my voice went thin and echoed. I heard her ask my name, but her voice was echoing too and my legs went all rubbery. I sat down hard on the floor and the room spun. The rain seeping over the window turned a funny blood colour. I shook my head and opened my eyes and the windows were still red. I was sitting inside the OMA and Yoona's voice came on the intercom.

'Stay inside, don't move. Decontaminating.'

We were in the exit port. It was closed, but Yoona still had on her space suit. The helmet was closed and I couldn't see her face. She waved a gloved hand at me to stay seated and I nodded.

I was still giddy. There was a horrible taste in my mouth and a sickly sweet smell in the air. Most of the red powder was gone now, sucked up overhead with a loud humming sound.

17

'You prexed.' Even on the intercom, her voice sounded unfriendly.

'How did you get me back?'

Yoona didn't reply. She was asking COL something, then came back on the intercom again. 'Clear reading.' She opened the cockpit cover and let me out.

'Yoona—'

'Not now. I want to get Deepwater moving.'

She pushed me to the airlocks. They opened and shut behind us. She didn't look at me or speak. Below deck she just took off her helmet and magnetic shoes. Then, still without speaking, she went upstairs.

She was in her control chair when I went up. I was back in my track suit, my head still hurt and that pollen smell in my nose made me sick. Deepwater was vibrating, moving very fast. I knew that Yoona was very angry with me, but I had to face that.

A print-out was flickering on the console. She looked at me. 'COL analysed the red stuff those trees were throwing off,' she said abruptly. 'An aid to digestion.'

I had nearly been eaten by a tree.

'How did you rescue me?'

'I used COL to override your control and put the OMA on automatic. Then I was able to get you in. Denie, you were very, *very* lucky.'

I knew that and I knew that only her quick thinking had saved my life. Deepwater was skimming very fast over the planet's surface. Most of it was rounded, green-blue hillocks of forest, speckled with red. Now they looked horrible and unwholesome.

'Deepwater is nearly recharged. We're leaving soon.'

We were coming to a break in the green-blue now. It was a thick band of the pollen stuff and seemed to be moving like a river in one direction. Red dust rose as we went over. Maybe the whole planet was alive, an entire monster

18

organism! I shivered. I must have looked pale, but the look Yoona gave me was stern and unforgiving.

'Understand very carefully, Cei.' In her anger she was using my ship name. 'What we are doing is too important to fail. Disobey me again and you will sleep in your casket the whole voyage.'

She meant every word of it, the way Mum did when she went public about her company dumping chemicals. And I knew better than to call Yoona's bluff. But no way was I taking *all* the blame.

'Then let's get our signals clear.' I was still scared, but getting angry. 'You told me to go out, you told me to look at those trees.'

'What?' she yelled and Deepwater jerked as though frightened. We were crossing a mountain range of green-blue spikes. 'Denie, I didn't even know you were gone!'

'I heard your voice. You opened the port!' I was scared again – I didn't understand why she was denying it.

'COL, were the airlocks and port opened before my last instruction?' she snapped.

'No memory,' came the cool-shadows voice.

'COL, what does "no memory" mean?' shouted Yoona. Robbie always said she was super-cool, but now she was angry and upset.

'No memory.'

'Yoona, maybe that voice was something from the planet . . . trying to get me out.' It was all I could think of. 'I swear I heard your voice.'

Her yellow eyes bored into me like a pair of lasers, but I looked straight back. Yoona sighed because she knew I was telling the truth.

'Sit down, and strap in.' I got into the chair beside her and Yoona ran her hand through her hair. 'Denie, this is bad. COL seems to be – doing things, then having memory blanks.'

She touched the crystals on the console like flicking worry

beads. There was another range now behind the first, of even bigger green-blue spikes, and Deepwater glided over it. Yoona spoke abruptly.

'Deepwater is a gene ark.' Below, another set of blue-green spikes whizzed by underneath. 'A cross-section of Earth-life ending at the lower primates.'

That was the secret of Deepwater! I just sat there as though all the air had been knocked out of me. Yoona was talking about Earth regenerating itself, about the half-million years it took Deepwater to time-circle the universe, how they returned to 'plant' their gene cargo like seed in a newly-ploughed field. And one word she used knocked all the air out of me again.

Returned!

'Yes, Denie.' She'd seen that look on my face. 'This is our second journey. We are going back to find the other Deepwater.'

There had not been one gene ark, but two. Robbie had told me about the wrecked twin ship they found drifting and abandoned in space. Not until it was too late, said Yoona, did they realise it held the other half of life on Earth – a gene bank of the human race.

So they were going back, across the black endless circle of the universe to find the other Deepwater and rescue its precious contents. Even to see if there was anything to rescue.

'We don't know,' said Yoona. 'We have to try.' A third, even taller range of green-blue mountains was looming ahead. 'Deepwater has already time-blinked halfway. So in life-terms we'll only be on the spaceship another six months.' She gave a wry smile. 'Most of that in deep sleep.'

'I . . . I think you're all fantastic.' It was the most incredible thing I had ever heard.

'We, Denie.' Yoona smiled again. 'You're part of Deepwater now.'

It was the best and most scary moment of my life. All I could do was sit there and start to breathe again as Yoona turned Deepwater to run alongside the range of giant turquoise spikes ahead. They were capped in white – flowers, not snow – and they were massive, many times bigger than anything on Earth. Even our steady spaceship was made small against them. Yoona spoke again.

'COL, have you completed recharging?'

'Yes.'

Yoona frowned, thinking hard about her next decision when a huge gap appeared in the spiked green-blue range. It stretched away on either side and she touched the controls, turning Deepwater to go through.

Our huge shadow followed us across the snow-flower slopes. It was wonderful how Yoona controlled Deepwater, as though she were part of it, as easily as I cornered my bike. The gap snaked through the mountains, kilometres wide, and Deepwater chased its own black shadow. We were flying very, very fast.

'Serious . . .' whispered Yoona and I knew she was thinking about COL again.

Could we trust it? We would go back into the caskets soon and we had to know COL would go on taking us in the right direction – and remember to wake us when ordered.

'Maybe it's a computer virus.' Mum had one of those and it ate all her data.

'After this many thousands of years?' Yoona shook her head.

'Something that came from the planet then?'

'I scanned. No trace if there was.' She bit her lip, very concerned. But she knew we had to trust COL, as there was no other choice. Yoona shrugged. 'COL . . .'

Ahead of us, the gap was flattening out into a thick green-blue jungle-hair. And suddenly it was cut by a huge round circle of yellow, a raw painful colour as though all the green had been scooped away.

'COL, forward bearing. I want that yellow circle on the vision screen.' There was a tense note to Yoona's voice.

21

She was turning Deepwater towards it and we moved quickly closer. The vision screen sprang into life. In the centre of the yellow was a row of round, black bubbles like igloos. Beside them, a tall black column and some long black things like snakes. We only had a second to look at them before COL spoke.

'Silicone-based life-readings.'

'COL, starboard variant eight!' Yoona jerked upright. 'COL, immediate vertical climb. We are leaving planet atmosphere – maximum speed!'

Deepwater went up in a steep climb. I made to speak, then saw something move on the vision screen. The yellow patch and black buildings were still there, in 3-D life, but two of the black 'snakes' were already slithering forward over the yellow surface. They stiffened and took off, jetting up like rockets. One minute they were on the ground, the next they were in the air.

'Yoona, I don't understand.'

'COL has screened this planet for indigenous life-forms.' She was speaking calmly, but was still very tense. 'There is nothing that is silicone-based.'

Outside, the blue atmosphere was already darkening. I tried to speak as calmly as Yoona and couldn't. 'They're . . . not from this planet either.'

'COL, full cruising speed,' said Yoona. 'No, Denie. They're aliens like us.'

On the vision screen, the two black snakes wriggled in a tight turn and came speeding up after us, as fast as Deepwater.

4   Space fight

Black space was closing all round Deepwater now and Yoona
kept the rate of climb very steep. Behind us, seen from our
vision screen, the two black snake-ships were moving just
as quickly. There was something really unpleasant about
the way they kept silently after us.

'Yoona . . . can't we time-blink?' I was trying not to sound
nervous, but those things were already closer.

'Not yet,' she said. 'Look what's ahead.'

That distant white circle I had seen over the sky was like
a huge band of broken space rock encircling the planet. It
was a bit like one of Saturn's rings. Some time in the long-
ago past, a moon had somehow broken up and then been
pulled close to a planet itself, scattering all round and as
dangerous as a minefield. Deepwater was already making
minor course corrections, as programmed, but any faster
and those rocks would be hitting us like express trains.

Now bigger rocks were tumbling round us like bowling
balls. Yoona's touch on the controls was light and sure. She
was flying Deepwater like a mobile skittle through a bowling
alley. I looked closer up at the vision screen. The black snake-
ships were nearer.

'COL, I want a monitor on those things.' She rattled out
their co-ordinates. 'Advise if they launch anything.'

'Confirm monitoring.'

Another huge chunk of sharp-edged space rock sailed
past, so close it nearly hit the window. Yoona snapped an
order.

'Denie, the bubble. Get on the laser cannon.'

'I've never fired that thing!' I yelled.

'Now is a good time to learn.' Another slight flick of the controls and I flinched as a monster lump zoomed overhead.

'Are you sure they want to make trouble?' I said, 'because I do believe in non-violence whenever possible and—'

'Denie, move!'

I moved. Up the spiral stairs and it was just how Robbie described it – like stepping on top of the spaceship. The bubble was a huge turret of clear iron-glass, enclosing the long twin barrels of the laser cannon. They were for blasting magnetic meteors and the Deepwater crew adapted them to fight off the alien horrors of Colour-space.

'Strap yourself in,' came Yoona's voice on the intercom.

I slipped into the big recliner couch under the gun controls. The cannon barrels stretched out before me and right overhead were two little star-craters in the iron-glass from a trite attack that Robbie had told me about. Trites, something else I hadn't met. Yoona's voice came through the intercom again.

'Can you see them?'

Yes, I could. Two snaky black shapes ducking and weaving through the rockfield, like they'd had plenty of practice. They were closer now and catching up fast.

'They're closer,' I said, actually managing to sound calm.

'Four controls on the cannon,' said Yoona. 'Look through the viewing scope. The far left crystal sets the scope and far right fires the cannon. Centre two for individual control, move the chair and the cannon moves, sighting is automatic to the scope – get it?'

'Got it.' It was simple all right, too simple.

'Track them,' she said.

I looked through the viewing scope. My feet were on pedals and I held handles on either side. The scope zapped up the black craft like they were coming down my throat.

Each had a long slit across the front like one heavy-lidded eye and another below like a frowning lip.

'Gaining,' I said.

'I know it.' Yoona's voice was tense. 'Ten minutes before we clear this belt.'

Ten minutes too long! They would be up to us by then and they looked dangerous. It was just in the way they followed, whiplashing round the rocks like a pair of black, hunting snakes. Then, something green spat from the mouth of one and a bullet-shaped spurt of green fire streaked towards us.

'COL reports missile fired,' came Yoona's calm voice. 'Blast it, Denie.'

Blast it? How? My hands wavered on the controls. The first crystal was scope-setting. I pressed it and a red sightline locked across the vision screen. Yoona's calm voice again, speaking quickly.

'On sight, the target will set in a circle. Fire at that point.' And she must have sensed my surge of trapped panic. 'Denie, we all need you now.'

Reb. Or Gret, Lis, Bren, the ones I hadn't met yet. They were all relying on me, and so was Deepwater itself. And I could feel the strong power of the spaceship flowing into me. I pressed my face closer to the scope and touched the crystal. Already the green fireball was getting bigger and bigger. I ran the sight over, it locked and I touched the second crystal.

The heavy thump of the cannon jolted me in my seat and two solid thin columns of yellow light zoomed out. I thumbed the crystal again and the lasers blasted like long yellow pencil marks into the blackness.

Nothing happened. It wasn't as easy as it looks in the video games. The laser bolts licked all round the green fireball and it kept coming.

'Rapid fire,' said Yoona.

No. I stopped a moment and took a deep breath. I had to stay calm; this was impossible, but it was happening. I

25

pressed my face into the vision screen again, the green fireball was almost filling it.

'Denie!' shouted Yoona.

Then the video circle locked and I thumbed the crystal hard. A yellow needle of laser hit the fireball and popped it like a balloon.

'Good shooting,' yelled the intercom happily.

The second black snake-ship had fired now. Feeling like a great woman warrior, I ran the gunsights over, waited, then thumbed the crystal again. The laser boomed and the green fireball popped into a mass of gasses.

Our two black hunters were stretched out at full speed now. They were watching us and not where they were going. One of them suddenly hit a lump of space rock and jerked round, stopping and dropping back as though hurt. The first black snake doubled back at once to cover it. They didn't try to fire again. They just waited as though they knew they'd lost and didn't mind being destroyed.

I still didn't know who or what those alien things were, but at least they stuck by each other. And now they were expecting to be blasted. I had the video sights on them, so a touch of the crystal was all it would take. They were finished.

I raised the sights a little and circled a chunk of rock tumbling over them, then fired. It exploded, scattering the two snakes with bits of rock. I think they got the message all right, for they ducked and began turning round.

'Next time wait for orders.' Yoona's voice had a touch of approval, though. I think that was how she would have handled it.

The green-blue planet was growing smaller and the alien base was just a yellow speck on the surface. The two snake-ships were lost in the blackness now and I was relieved. I had no idea what silicone-based life forms looked like and didn't want to find out.

'That place looked like some kind of mining colony,' I said.

Maybe that was why the planet fought us. It thought we were miners too, stripping off its fresh green-blue and leaving that raw yellow underneath. And I remembered the moving river of red pollen we had seen. If that was on its way to the alien camp, they had a horrible surprise coming.

'Maybe,' said Yoona, after a long pause. 'COL reports no pursuit. Come down.'

I unstrapped myself. My body ached from the tight pressure of the straps and the boom-boom of the laser had given me a headache. I don't know how Lis ever blasted her way through whole shoals of magnetic meteors. I went down and collapsed in a chair beside Yoona. There was deep black space all round now and I breathed a sigh of relief.

'Free again,' I said.

Yoona gave me a curious look. 'Is that how you feel?'

I nodded and wriggled a bit in my seat. I was still tired, but there was something soothing and beautiful in how deep space was opening up round us, as though we and Deepwater belonged and were part of it.

'Yes, I feel like I was made for all this.'

Yoona smiled. 'You were. We all were.'

I looked beside me. Yoona's hands were lightly on the controls, her blonde and red hair falling carelessly round her shoulders. She looked strong and assured, like she could control any situation at all. Pity Meatgrinder if he flicked a pellet at her. Outer space was Yoona's life and she was a free spirit in this black solar jungle.

We sat there for minutes on end. I forgot about the double existence I was leading, the lab and that Ms Orduna, even home. It all seemed a distant irritating memory that should be forgotten as soon as possible. Then COL made a minor course change and broke the spell.

'COL, are we linked back on course?'

'Yes.'

'Are you ready for time-blink?'

'Yes.'

27

Yoona hesitated, and the worried note came back into her voice. 'COL, have you traced any record of those missing instructions?'

'Memory banks scanned. Nothing.' COL might have been telling us the time of day instead of admitting a serious fault.

And we had to accept it. Two-thirds of the voyage still lay ahead of us. Anybody who stayed on deck, even at time-blinking speed, would be a few hundred years older when we reached Colour-space. Yoona had no choice and she knew it.

'COL, I am setting time-blink for one hour from now. Confirm please.'

'Time-blink one hour, confirmed.'

Yoona unstrapped herself. She was still wearing her space suit. She reached inside and pulled out the little disc she wore round her neck.

'I want you to hear this, Denie.'

She pressed the sides and the disc spoke in a woman's tired voice. Yoona's mother was one of the first crew when Deepwater took off from Mars in 2090; she had left this message behind for her daughter. It was not long and spoke of love and goodbyes – and no more mistakes with their home planet of Earth. My own eyes were full of tears when it finished.

'You see how important all this is?' I nodded and Yoona slipped the disc back into her tunic. 'I've got some wrap-up on the programme. Then we'll go down to the caskets.'

'I'll wait below, Yoona.' I could sense she wanted to be on her own up here for a time. She smiled and I went down the stairs.

Already I had the feeling that Deepwater was home. I remembered that sense of stalking terror when I first woke up. Maybe it was just nerves, as I couldn't feel it now. But it was strange to think that soon I would be falling asleep for hundreds of Earth-time years, while Deepwater time-blinked

28

millions of years, space-time. Or if COL glitched again, then we would all sleep forever – but I had to put that out of my mind. Yoona came down.

'Ready?' she said. The lights went out on the upper deck as she spoke and the hatch slid shut.

'Ready.'

We went silently together down the long corridor, our boots tapping on the metal floor. The automatic lights came on again, pushing back the darkness and closing it behind us. The door to the NUN chamber was open. No sensation of terror now. Just a huge cool semi-darkness. Once this giant room had blazed with golden power generated by its super bio-computer, NUN. Now the terminal-globe hung overhead, shattered and dead, and the room was quiet. We walked up to the row of crystal caskets. I knew them all now; they were all heroes.

BREN was the name on the first base-plate. From Ceres, a midway asteroid colony between Mars and Jupiter, he was a tall, tough young miner with hair in dark red dreadlocks. He didn't like Robbie or Yoona, but once he took Deepwater into the tornado of an exploding spaceship to rescue them. They didn't like Bren either – but they would have done the same.

Beside Bren was GRET. A green-haired, green-eyed North Martian girl with smarts enough for them both. She had lost one eye in a trite attack and now it was covered by a black patch. She and Yoona disliked each other, but with the respect of equals.

An open casket – Yoona's. Then REB, Robbie's space-name. I could only see a pale blur of features under the thick slab of rain-crystal. He and Yoona nearly lost their lives unlocking the secrets of Deepwater. And the Earth-side of Robbie had no memory of this, the space-side.

LIS. Blue-haired, yellow-eyed and stubborn as a little bulldog. Time after time, her skill with the laser cannon had saved Deepwater from the trites and amebs. Another

29

North Martian (North-*West*, Lis would say), but fiercely loyal to Yoona.

And beside her, ZAK. He had lost his life in the last battle with NUN. So they had put him back in his casket, hoping that would keep a spark in his body, that some unknown process of Deepwater would keep him alive and one day wake him up.

Yoona let me stand there until I was ready. I only had to lie down on my padded couch – it was very simple. It worked somehow on sonics and a nutrient light flow. The pressure of my own bodyweight made something hum and I lifted my hand to Yoona.

'See you next time round?'

'All right, Denie.'

No goodbyes – neither of us wanted that. A delicious melting soundwave was flowing through my body and I shut my eyes as the crystal cover closed overhead. Everything sank down into a peaceful darkness.

Then I was awake again, with my eyes still closed. It felt like I was in a different bed and I opened them, into a different room. White ceilings, white walls and a strange light.

5 Blackout

Everything seemed unreal, but before I had time to be scared I looked sideways and there was my dad asleep in a chair – looking more like a long-haired English sheepdog than ever.

'Dad?' I said.

He opened his eyes. Then things happened so quickly that I had to shut mine again. A doctor and some nurses came in and Dad kept blinking as though his eyes hurt, squeezing my hand tight and saying I was OK, OK. Then Mum came in, crying. It seemed I'd been in hospital two weeks and they'd taken it in turns to sit with me.

I'd passed out at the lab. So they got me to the hospital and although there was nothing wrong, I just didn't wake up. For two weeks! The doctor gave me a few tests and said I needed rest. After sleeping fourteen days? Mum and Dad wanted to stay and be very quiet, but they were shooed away. I felt really bad about what I'd put them through. They were both very busy and had taught me to be independent. Sometimes I felt a bit left out of their lives. But we did care for each other and for *two weeks* I had put them through the wringer.

I had no idea why I passed out for so long. Earth-time and Deepwater-time were crazily different – Robbie found that out, too – but it still seemed too long. Maybe it was because my space-side was sleeping in that casket. It gave me a really strange feeling to think of being somewhere in the future, in space, billions of kilometres away.

I was kept in for two days more for observation, and

31

Mum and Dad just about lived in my room. Mum even gave up her squash night and Dad let me beat him at chess. They were really concerned because the hospital couldn't explain my medical condition. Neither could I. Prexing, Deepwater, alien planets and snake-ships? They would have put me in another kind of hospital room – one with padded walls.

And Robbie came to see me! He sidled in with a bunch of grapes (half of them eaten), and said not to worry about the bike, as he'd got it back OK. He ended up staying a long time and we talked a lot. I wanted to because he was a link with Deepwater, with pale features under rain-crystal and a REB name plate. I think a very hidden part of him, deep down, knows we are much closer than just being friends. But the other ninety-nine per cent is very puzzled.

On my last day, Chibbi Orduna arrived. She had on purple cord trousers, a bright poncho with orange and red stripes and a wide-brimmed black hat with a silver band. She grinned at me like we were old friends. 'I brought some stuff for you to read,' she said. 'All about genes.'

'Thanks. I hope I didn't scare you, passing out like that.'

'Scare me?' she laughed. 'Kid, I freaked out!' She changed the subject. 'Would you like to have a talk with me sometime – a real talk?'

'Yes, I would,' I said.

'You seem very interested in genes.' She still smiled but her eyes went cool and deep. 'So am I.' I nodded, not wanting to give anything away. We chatted a while, then she got up to go. 'By the way – Yoona?'

What did she know about Yoona? I must have muttered something when I passed out. And how much had I said? 'Yoona?' I tried to sound puzzled. 'What does that mean?'

'You don't remember saying it?' The cool deep look was back in her eyes.

'No, Ms Orduna.'

'Call me Chibbi.' The look went and she laughed again.

32

'Where does your name come from?' Good move, Denie, I thought, change the subject. I offered her some grapes.

'It's Hindu.' She popped a grape in her mouth and grinned. 'From my godmother in Bombay, India. Mum and Dad are travelling nuts, they never stop. Never will.'

'What about the Orduna part?'

She ate some more grapes. 'My folks are Irish-American and Mexican-Spanish. I'm somewhere in the middle.'

'*¿Habla usted Español?*' I said. Three years in Central America made it my second language.

'*Si, si*, I speak Spanish, *chica!*' and I was a good kid because I made her forget about Yoona. She got up to go. 'So call me Chibbi.'

'I will. I never heard that name before.'

'I never heard Yoona.'

'You wouldn't, it's . . .' my tongue tied into a knot ' . . . but I don't know anyone called Yoona.'

'None of your girlfriends?' She was quick, cool and deep, very casual.

'No.'

'OK, must run.' She got up to go. 'See you soon?'

'Yes,' I said. She grinned again and left.

I never wanted to play chess with Chibbi! Irish, Mexican and Spanish must make a very clever mix in the gene-blender. I'd admitted Yoona was a name – after saying I didn't know. *And* a girl's name. So how much else had I sleep-talked in my prex? I would have to be very careful with her and keep my lip buttoned tight. She was just too sharp.

Mum and Dad took me home that afternoon. In telling my story, this is what I call my 'burn-out time'. I felt empty inside, like a drained torch battery. Mum had painted my room and Dad made a great French dinner. But on my first night, I had that Deepwater dream again. I was back on the upper deck, just as I remembered it, in darkness and with an evil, hating presence in the cold

33

black shadows. I woke up suddenly and had to bite my lip to stop crying out.

I had another problem, Earth-side, too. Meatgrinder and Reeboks had me targeted. In the first three days back at school, I had my books superglued, beetles in my lunch box and my hockey stick went missing. I had to deal with them. It's like Mum says, non-violence is one thing but never let anyone walk all over you. So I made my plans and blast-off hour was 8.30 a.m. on my fourth day back at school.

Mum and Dad were still very worried. They thought it was some kind of nervous trauma and took it in turns to have little heart-to-hearts with me. They wouldn't pressure me and that helped because I couldn't tell them. The Deepwater secret was locked in me like computer data needing the right password; so far, nobody had spoken it.

On day four, I left early and made my preparations. Then I biked round to where Meatgrinder lives. His mum runs a little dairy and video game parlour and it was open already. She was there, a big woman in a pink jumper and purple track suit pants, yelling at him to get to school. He came out and I biked up to him.

'Hi, Connal.' Meatgrinder had invented his own nickname and I refused to use it.

He just scowled and looked round.

'So what now, Connal? More books superglued? Do I get my hockey stick back?'

'I never took that!' he yelled, and it sounded true. Did Reeboks steal it on his own? He tried to move and I blocked him. 'Get out of my way!'

He pushed his bike up to mine, but he wasn't shouting too loud and I realised why. His mum would hear him, maybe come out and learn all about his little stunts. I think Meatgrinder was scared of his mum.

'You're letting Reeboks use you,' I said. 'I don't want any problems. Can't we be friends?'

34

'Eh?' He scowled. I think it was the only facial expression he knew.

'Or shall we just leave each other alone?'

Meatgrinder scowled again, then an empty soft-drink can clanged on my handlebars.

'Yeah, then spill your guts to dear Mizz Booby, like you did before.' Reeboks was behind me, his voice high and taunting.

Meatgrinder's mouthpiece had arrived, so further communication was down the tubes. Meatgrinder rammed his bike up to mine. I spun round and headed off. They began following just as I knew they would, one on either side. I tried just once more.

'Connal, you don't have to be a jerk!'

'You're just a girl and girls are good for one thing,' said Meatgrinder.

'Yes, what's that?' I didn't even turn round.

He told me. Even if I repeated the word, I couldn't repeat the crude leer that went with it. Reeboks squealed with delight. 'Meaty-boy, you made the little girly blush!'

'You've got a real hang-up, you pint-sized creep!' I yelled back. Sure my face was red, but that happens when I'm getting mad! Meatgrinder put on speed to lean over and slap my bottom hard. Oh, did I want to smash them both! But I'd made my plans. I kept going and let my hot temper boil into a cold, icy rage.

They followed, giggling to each other. Reeboks was the puppet-master, I was sure, pulling Meatgrinder's vocal strings. So my plan had to get rid of both of them. I turned off the street, down a path, into the park.

They followed, thinking I was trying to get away. I put on some speed and so did they. I heard Reeboks mutter something about the creek, which was shallow and very muddy. Oh yes, I thought, nice one, Reeboks – push me into it, eh? But I was way ahead of them. I broadsided round a corner and put on more speed. The track wound up and down, over a narrow footbridge. I jerked the bike up, jumped the first part and kept going.

Reeboks and Meatgrinder were just behind and both put on speed to be first over. So their bike wheels met where the bridge started – where some unknown hand had rubbed soap over the wood. The two bikes skidded. It was really interesting to watch how Meatgrinder and Reeboks came together then apart again, like flower petals opening into the sunlight – one over each side of the bridge, into the mud.

It was pure joy to see just how much a few centimetres of mud can totally enslime the human body. Or in this case, two human bodies. I stood looking at the two mud-monsters wallowing in their just deserts and grinned. But I couldn't grin for very long – I even felt a bit ashamed of myself. I'd always told myself I was better than them – then I'd pulled exactly the same low trick.

'You're not the only ones who can pull dirty tricks,' I shouted and that made it even worse. I was admitting to myself that it *was* a dirty trick – me, Denie, the great pacifist – and putting myself on the same level as Reeboks.

Mud-Meatgrinder spat out some green weeds and the two of them began slopping about. Mud-Reeboks was on his hands and knees and they didn't look at me. I kicked some earth over the soapy patch and went back to my bike. I was tired and somehow breathless, and my legs felt wobbly. Maybe I shouldn't have done all that, so soon after coming out of hospital. I went over and sat down on a bench.

Mud-Reeboks was pulling his bike out. 'You're going to get into trouble over this!' he wailed.

'Are you going to steal my tennis racket this time?' I yelled.

Mud-Meatgrinder shot a look at Mud-Reeboks, again as though he didn't know anything about that. I didn't care – I was tired and lay down on the hard, wooden bench. It almost seemed comfortable. Then my head spun and I knew what

36

was happening, but it was too late. I jerked round and turned over, opening my eyes. And the first thing I saw was a crystal cover lifting and the broken remains of the NUN terminal-globe overhead.

I was back on Deepwater.

6   Unseen enemy

The reality of Deepwater was sudden and intense. My eyes
were gummy and my legs felt weak as I sat up. But straight
away I had the same feeling Robbie had talked about – that
everything Earth-side was only a dream, even my parents.
All the other caskets were open except Zak's, of course, and
the eighth one beside me, which had never opened.
Deepwater was humming with life and seemed to be moving
very fast. Then somebody called.

'Are you all right?'

A girl in a space suit walked up. She was short and a
little tubby. Her helmet visor was open, showing a blue face
and big yellow eyes like a cat's. She had short, blue hair,
yellowed at the ends, and I knew her name. Lis.

'Awake, Yoona,' she said into the helmet intercom. She
had a laser rifle slung over her shoulder.

'I'm all right,' I said.

'Everyone else is on deck.' She was looking at me in a
stiff, strange way. 'You have to put a space suit on.'

'Why?'

'Yoona will tell you.' Even her voice sounded stiff and
she watched in silence while I put on the space suit and
helmet. Sometimes she looked round, a hand touching the
rifle, as though expecting trouble.

'Why the rifle?' I asked.

'Yoona will tell you.' She looked round again and I
realised she was on edge – expecting something to happen?
She was standing by Zak's casket and I realised that might

be part of her stiffness. Lis and Zak were a team and now a stranger – me – had replaced him. I was a reminder that he was gone and she didn't like that.

'I'm missing a glove,' I said. I looked round but it was nowhere.

She shrugged. 'Never mind. Come on.'

She led the way as quickly as her metal-soled boots allowed her. I followed, still dazed, but all this was already so natural and real.

'What did Robbie say about me?'

Lis glanced back. 'What was *Reb* supposed to say?' She stressed the 'Reb' part very obviously.

So Yoona hadn't told the others I was an Earth-gene too. Why not? Lis was heading for the door and into that long, long corridor, still looking round, one hand on her rifle. All the way down, she didn't look at me once. Deepwater might be natural to me, but I was still a stranger to its crew.

We went through to the below deck. Yoona was coming down the stairs and Lis went on past and up them, leaving us alone. 'Hello, Cei,' she said.

'Denie . . . please?'

She nodded with a tight smile. She was wearing her space suit and also had a laser rifle slung over her shoulder.

'Yoona, what's wrong?'

'Nothing should be wrong.' She unslung her rifle and laid it on a bunk. 'COL woke me up on time, we are on course and Colour-space is just ahead.'

'Then what is it? What happened?'

Yoona set her lips in a tense line. 'Denie, did you have dreams, bad dreams about something evil hating you?'

'Yes,' I whispered.

'We all did. I think there is something on Deepwater that hates us. Something strong enough to get into our minds and even worse.'

'What happened?' I whispered, and that feeling of

40

nightmare came back with her answer.

'It tried to kill us.'

Yoona had set her casket to open first. She left the NUN
chamber at once, shutting the airtight door. And it was lucky
she did. Because as she opened the door to the lower deck,
both exit ports and all the airlocks opened, flooding both
decks of Deepwater with black, cold space. She should have
been dead, sucked out into space with all the air. But Yoona
remembered the last time that the airlocks had opened on
their own. She closed the ports and airlocks manually and
when COL came back on stream, air pressure and
Deepwater's artificial gravity were restored.

'COL has no memory – again.' She looked tired and
concerned. 'I think something else opened those airlocks.'

'Something alien from the planet?' I said. 'Through the
port or side-vents?'

'COL scanned again – nothing.' Yoona sighed. 'So we
wear our space suits until this is sorted out. Now come and
meet the others – except Reb.'

I was filled with panic. 'Where is he – did something
happen?'

'Out in the OMA, checking the hull.' She gave a little
smile. 'It'll be a nice surprise when you meet.'

I had to grin myself. It would be a nice *big* surprise
because Reb had all his Robbie Mikkelson Earth-gene
memories. We went on deck.

Lis had gone on up to the bubble. There were two kids in
the control chairs and Yoona introduced us, but I already
knew their names, Gret and Bren, because there was no
mistaking those colours.

'Hi,' I said, but they just looked at me as though I was
something in a shop window.

'Don't go near any airlocks.' Bren was just as Robbie
had described him, down to the dark red dreadlocks and
cold, teasing grin.

'Are you blaming me for what happened on that planet?' I said incredulously.

'Bren's idea of a joke,' said Yoona, but neither Bren nor Gret was even smiling.

The other one, Gret, was still looking at me in silence. She had a sharp, clever face, green skin, green hair and a black eye patch. Her one green eye flickered as though she'd seen me somewhere, then her lips set in a tight, sour line. I walked up and put my hand out. They just kept looking at me.

'Don't they shake hands on North Mars?' I said, trying to smile. It was like the first day in a new school.

'Why, are you going to teach us manners?' said Gret in a very sour-polite way, adding softly, 'Earthkid.'

'I'd rather do something useful,' I said. If this was how they wanted it, then OK. 'And if we're going to start calling each other names, then I know some too. Like sandbrain.'

North Martians do *not* like being called that! Bren got up out of his chair, but Gret pulled him back. Her one eye blazed green. 'You just prove yourself, that's all,' she hissed.

'All right, all right, exchange of courtesies over.' Yoona kept her voice smooth and her mouth straight. 'Denie will be pairing with Lis.'

'You and Reb keep voice-ac to COL, of course!' snapped Gret.

'Yes.' Yoona's voice went hard.

'This time we want to know everything *when* it happens.' Bren stood up again. 'Not after Earthkids get to hear about us.'

'And this time you're going to obey orders,' said Yoona in a voice like two meteors grating together.

'The way she did on that planet?' said Gret.

I could not believe any of this. These kids had taken their spaceship through a deep space minefield of unknown dangers, risked their lives for each other a dozen times and

42

were doing it again. And they were still fighting each other – like kids.

'Bubble, Denie,' said Yoona, turning her back on them. 'COL, maintain holding pattern.' She led the way up.

At the top, Lis was checking the laser controls with quick, sure movements. She didn't look like she'd been asleep for several hundred years.

'You and Denie will spell each other, Lis.' Lis kept checking and nodded without looking up. A voice came through on the ship's intercom.

'No sign of hull damage, no sign of forced entry through the vent-filters or exhaust locks.' The last time I heard that voice was at the hospital when Robbie was telling me it was OK about his bike.

'Reb, our new wake-up's on deck,' said Yoona.

'OK.' He sounded like he didn't care. That made me annoyed. I could take rudeness from the others, but if Robbie Mikkelson tried then he was in trouble.

'Look,' said Yoona.

It was fantastic standing in the turret. The iron-glass was so clear, it was like standing in a water-bubble. Ahead, across the black distance, were twinkling spots and clumps of colour, among them the frozen red explosion of a nova – an exploded star.

'Colour-space,' said Yoona.

Even twenty-first century solar exploration had known almost nothing about Colour-space. It was just too far away – hundreds of earth lifetimes – and a jungle of the unknown. Alien creatures, weird and dangerous space formations and solunks, the black solar icebergs. So mysterious, so dangerous that both Deepwaters had to clone crews to take them through it. Us.

But one Deepwater hadn't made it. So we were on our way back to try and save the gene cargo. COL had said it was almost indestructible so we had a chance – a very slim chance.

43

'Has Yoona told you about the trites?' Lis said suddenly. She was polishing the viewing-scopes and pointed up at the two star-craters in the dome. 'They nearly got in once. They lay their eggs in you, then you die.' She took a blue biscuit out of her pocket and began eating it.

Trites. Deadly and super-fast space insects with drill-stings that could penetrate anything except the silver-plate hull of Deepwater. They were named after underground insects on Mars that drilled into solid stone to lay their eggs and chances were they did the same thing here.

'And amebs,' said Lis. 'They're like monster jellyfish. They can take any colour and shape and most times you can't even screen them. Once they get hold of Deepwater . . .' She finished by biting her biscuit in half and crunching it noisily.

I began to realise what was going on. I was the new kid and this was my first day of school. Lis was telling me the way it was. And she was off-hand because I still had to prove myself. Yoona had stood to one side, watching us and not speaking.

'You'll have to teach me a lot,' I said.

'And you'd better learn quickly,' said Lis.

'Denie's had one lesson,' said Yoona. 'She scared off two alien spaceships at that planet stop.'

Lis looked at me for the first time and her big yellow eyes went a bit rounder. Yoona beckoned me. 'Denie can tell you about it later,' she said.

'Yes,' said Lis, her eyes still round.

We went back down to the main deck, the metal boots clanging with every step. I was hot already, but we had to wear the suits and helmets until the airlocks were secure. Gret and Bren were still in their chairs and neither of them turned.

'We're going to weld bolts on the airlock doors when Robbie has docked,' said Yoona. 'So they can't open automatically.'

44

'And hope there's no more jel,' said Bren. His hand went up to tug a dreadlock, but he couldn't because they were tucked in his helmet.

'The jel was part of NUN's bio-mass,' said Yoona. 'And NUN is gone.'

'Now, we have another enemy.' Gret looked at me with a little smile I didn't like.

Yoona headed for her control chair. 'Denie, go below and say hello to Reb.'

Now it had come, I felt a little scared at the thought. Gret muttered something about Earthkids comparing prexes and Bren gave that little whistle of his. All part of a little game they played, always testing, always pushing – and one step away from being serious.

I went below. The space suit was very hot and I still felt a bit numb. The metal-soled boots hurt my feet and I sat down, deciding it wouldn't hurt to unstrap them while I waited for Reb. The lights dimmed as I thought of it. Then I suddenly had that feeling of something unseen, watching and hating me. Something from those bad dreams! I stood up, the lights dimmed again and a vibration shook the lower deck.

'Close helmets!' I heard Yoona scream.

In the same moment, the airlocks slid open. I slammed my visor down and grabbed for my boots. Too late. The air was being sucked out, snatching me with greedy fingers down the airlock tunnel and out of the port into deep, black space.

7 The enemy takes shape

It was so sudden and horrible, I didn't even have time to yell for help. One moment I was on Deepwater, the next hurtling through the open port like a rag doll shot from a cannon. Then a bug-eyed monster grabbed me and a voice spoke in my helmet.

'Got you.'

The claws were steel, gently nipping my wrist and ankle. The bug-eyed monster was the OMA with a helmeted figure in the cockpit. Reb had been about to re-enter when he met me coming out and did his best catch ever. 'Relax and breathe, we'll get back all right.'

And Yoona's voice was buzzing in my helmet. 'Power restored, maintain emergency procedure inside.'

Reb was holding me like a puppy is held by the scruff of its neck. He was still calm, as though this happened every day.

'Be more careful next time, Cei.'

He was steering the OMA round, back into the port and the circular door began closing out the cold blackness of space. He settled the OMA on the deck, still holding me. All right, he was Reb now, not Robbie, but I was going to use his Earth-name just once more. I had to make a joke or go mad!

'Robbie, the Principal says if you miss another easy goal like in that match against Pasadena, he'll bust you down to the juniors.'

He yelled and the claws holding me jerked up and down.

The port was shut and Yoona's voice – very smooth – came through the intercom. 'Reb, I forgot to mention the new wake-up, Cei, has the Earth-name Denie Miles. I think you know each other.'

'Denie Miles?' He yelled into the intercom.

'Yes, Mikkelson, Chibbi Orduna took *both* our genes. Let me down!'

'Who the hell is Chibbi Orduna?' he shouted.

'Let me down and I'll tell you,' I shouted back. I could hear someone laughing on the intercom – Lis, I think.

Reb opened the pincers and dumped me like a sack of potatoes. He scrambled out and pulled me up. I could see his eyes behind the glass now, and his mouth, opening and shutting like a fish.

'Denie . . . ?'

'Hi, Robbie – I mean Reb. Chibbi Orduna is the woman at that gene place. She's a good person.'

COL was back on-stream. The airlocks opened and shut behind us and Reb didn't speak again until we were back in the lower deck. Then we opened our visors.

'You've got red hair now,' he said.

'You would notice that first,' I answered.

He was still staring at me as though I didn't exist as Yoona's voice came on the intercom. 'Denie, your boots – and keep them on.' Then he gave a headshake like pulling himself together and knelt down to help me. The hatch slid open and Lis came staggering down with welding equipment nearly as big as herself.

'What's this sport you're not very good at, Reb?' she said too innocently and kept going. Reb gave me a look and pulled on the other boot. I looked back, but in a different way.

He was just like the Earth-Robbie. His skin was a nice goldy-brown and his black hair had a streak of red-blue. But there was a strength in his face that wasn't the same. Something seemed to register and he suddenly grinned, looking a lot more like the Earth-Robbie.

'Denie.' He said it as though the name was strange on his lips, but he grinned again and I felt a lot better, as though I'd found a new friend.

We talked for a little time while Lis soldered a heavy bolt on to the airlock door. *That* was not going to happen again, unless we wanted it to. Reb told me more about prexing – I'd have five or six before I said goodbye to Earth. And he didn't ask anything about school or his home even though he wanted to. It was all behind him, and he was doing the job he was cloned for, second-in-command on a star-voyaging gene ark.

We went back upstairs. Yoona was seated at her console and Robbie slipped into the chair beside her. 'COL's OK again?' he asked.

Yoona nodded. 'We can't go into Colour-space until this is sorted out,' she said.

Gret was sitting on the side of Bren's chair. He was whistling softly and had a dreadlock pulled out so he could tug it. Yoona gave me a stern look, her eyes flashing like yellow diamonds.

'Denie, did you touch the airlock controls?'

'No!'

Bren whistled again and tugged his dreadlock. Gret blinked her one green eye. They chose not to believe me, but I think Yoona did. She ran her hands through her blonde and red hair.

'COL has no memory of doing it, either,' she said.

So the unseen enemy was still among us.

Lis spent an hour welding the bolt on to the airlock door. Reb, Yoona, Bren and Gret checked all the controls through the ship, and each time COL told them (in cool-shadows boredom) that no false instructions were on record. I sat up in the bubble and tracked the laser cannon round in a circle, although there were no dangers – yet. Just me, going in a circle and thinking about enemies we could not see. Deepwater was in a holding pattern and the lights of Colourspace lay in the distance like a far-off city.

When Lis finished, Yoona called us back together. She told us there was nothing wrong – nothing we could find – and repeated screenings showed no alien presence. If there was something on Deepwater, then it must be hidden. Deepwater was a very big spaceship and there were still parts we knew nothing about – such as where COL's terminal was. So, Yoona said, we would keep wearing our space suits and always be on our guard. While she spoke, Gret watched me in that careful, green-eyed way of hers with the not-nice smile on her lips.

'Remember your dream about standing here on the upper deck?' she said with that sour-polite way of speaking.

'Yes.' I nodded. 'But it was just a bad dream.'

'We all had dreams about Deepwater,' said Reb.

'Yes Reb, we did.' Gret gave that not-nice smile of hers again. 'But Denie dreamed she was up here – on the control deck.'

'It was a dream,' I said. I was getting scared because there was something about her tone of voice.

'Or sleep-walking?' she said.

'Sleep-walking?' said Reb.

'Yes!' Her green eyes gleamed. 'Maybe that's how the airlocks opened. Maybe she did it, sleep-walking out of her casket.'

'Gret, none of us could do that,' said Yoona.

'No?' Her hand went under the seat and came up, holding something. 'Then explain this.' She threw down a glove with a black-lettered 'C' on the back.

There was no mistaking that 'C'. It stood for Cei and was mine. I even remembered missing it when I put on the space suit by the wake-up casket. Lis remembered, too – it showed in her face.

Gret was pleased with the reaction she'd produced.

50

'Yoona, you were the last to leave. Was the glove here then?'

Yoona gave Gret a look of dislike, but shook her head.

'I didn't leave it here.' My voice sounded tired and seemed to echo in my head. It was suddenly cold. The lights dimmed, everything flickering like a bad video image.

'All you Earthkids are useless while you're prexing,' said Bren.

'Shut up!' shouted Reb and took a step towards him. Bren was on his feet at once, fists clenching.

'Both of you shut up,' snapped Yoona. 'Cei, go and lie down, you're tired.' Cei, not Denie. She was being formal again.

'I'm all right.' But I was muttering to myself.

'You're not, you're going through a prex cycle,' said Reb. 'And you nearly got sucked into space. Go and lie down.'

'So you can all talk about me?' I shouted, angrily, because I could sense the disbelief.

'Hey, Denie . . .'

I shook off Reb's hand and clanged off down the hatch, stamping very hard on the deck button. The hatch slid shut behind me, and I sat down. I wished right then I could prex back to planet Earth forever. Did they really think I was causing all this?

I sat for several minutes, getting more and more upset. I didn't want to prex out of Deepwater forever – and that sudden zap into outer space had scared me a hell of a lot. Was I some kind of bad luck hoodoo?

'Oh, hell, what am I doing here?' I said aloud. The lights dimmed.

'Denie?'

Reb was there. I hadn't heard the hatch open or close. The lights dimmed again and made his face look pale and anxious.

'I made a really stupid fool of myself up there, didn't I?'

He shook his head. 'Nobody thinks you caused all this.' Reb was always nice. 'Yoona thinks you should rest.'

51

'All right.' I lay back.

'In your casket, Denie.'

I sat up again. I couldn't believe what I'd just heard! 'You want me back in – in deep sleep again?'

'Just for a time, Denie, until we're in Colour-space.' He was speaking slowly and awkwardly like he was very embarrassed. 'Until we get things sorted out.'

'And see if these things happen when I'm not here?'

Reb looked unhappy but stood there firmly. No, there was little of the Earth-Robbie in him, he was as cold as his bossy commander. All right then, maybe they were right, maybe I was a cuckoo in the nest. I was tired, my head was starting to pound and all I wanted to do was sleep.

I nodded. 'If that's what you want.'

He helped me off with my space suit. He wasn't wearing his either, so Yoona must have thought we were safe with the airlock doors bolted. I followed him back down that long passage.

Reb walked quickly. The lights were flickering here, too, and Deepwater no longer felt safe. Now it was a ship of strange happenings. I felt like I was being led to execution.

'You don't know I'm causing all this.'

'This is our way of finding out.' He walked quietly and lightly, his boots making almost no sound. Not like mine shuffling heavily behind.

'Shouldn't you wear your space suits until you know?' I said.

'We're safe,' he replied without turning round. In other words, they had already made up their minds.

We were at the NUN chamber now. Reb pressed his palm into the circle imprint and the door swung open. I walked through and it shut behind us, like a coffin lid closing. We went over to the caskets.

I blinked, my head buzzing. 'How long am I staying here?'

'We haven't decided.' It was strange the way he spoke, almost without moving his lips.

'I have the right to know.'

'Get in the casket, Denie.' His eyes glittered and the light reflected off his face in a pattern of thousands of tiny dots.

'How long, Reb?'

His lips moved but he didn't answer. He just looked at me and his eyes shone strangely.

'All right then, I'll ask Yoona.'

I made to move and he caught my wrist. His hand gripped tight, as cold and smooth as plastic. I pushed him and suddenly my hand sunk into his chest. It was a horrible feeling, like cold slime! I pulled it out and instead of blood, a patch of glittering dots appeared. This thing wasn't Reb!

'In . . . the . . . casket.'

His voice was a harsh croak like a tape running on flat batteries. And his face was slipping like jelly into something twisted and horrible. He croaked again.

'Cas . . . ket.'

It was a hideous sound! The Reb-thing held me tightly in that cold, smooth grip. I screamed and tried to pull back, but my headache exploded and the whole chamber began a mad spin. I felt myself being pushed back against the hard edges of the casket. I struggled and tried to tear my hand loose and heard the voice again.

'Hey, stoppit!'

A different voice.

8 *More trouble*

Something hard and knobbly was digging into my back, but the hand holding mine was taken away. I opened my eyes and coughed in the smoke. There was a pattern of sunlight and leaves on the ground and an opened can of soft drink. The knobbly thing was still digging in my back and I moved.

I was sitting up against a tree. There was a little fire going, just dry leaves and twigs, smoking more than burning. On the other side sat the last person in the world I expected to see.

Meatgrinder.

His hair was up in stiff spikes, his face and clothes smeared with mud. He was scowling at me, but Meatgrinder always scowled. Reeboks was nowhere to be seen. My bike was leaning against the bench and the sun was high overhead. It must be noon.

'I didn't hurt you,' he said hastily. 'Wasn't me that made you get knocked out like that.'

'I know.' I felt awful.

He offered me the can of soft drink, but I shook my head. It was still pounding and I had that horrible unreal feeling – of being suddenly back in a whole different life. And I could still see that horrible slipping face and feel the cold plastic hand on my wrist. 'What are you doing here, then?'

Meatgrinder was a boy of few words because when you took away the rude ones, a few was all he had left. So it took a lot of questions. He'd seen me faint – prex – and although Reeboks wouldn't stay, he did. He propped me up against the tree, lit the fire and tried to dry his clothes. Then he waited for me to open my eyes. He scowled again.

'I just don't want you getting me into hassles, that's all.'

'I didn't. Why do you believe everything Reeboks tells you?'

'He's my mate,' scowled Connal, without really answering.

'He stole my hockey stick – right?'

'Dunno,' he scowled again. But he did know.

'And you didn't pressure kids into using that crummy little video shop?'

Meatgrinder chucked some earth on the fire and stamped his foot down hard. 'It's not crummy, it's Mum's. She has to work all the time. So I got her more business.'

This conversation was as unreal as that Robbie-thing on Deepwater. The memory of that made me wince, so I stood up and so did Meatgrinder. His scowl became more uncertain.

'Are you going to tell on me?'

'No. You keep out of my way and I'll keep out of yours.'

'Yeah.'

'Thanks for staying,' I said.

He just scowled again and rode off, the mud cracking all over his body, looking like some Stone Age native covered with war paint.

I stood by the bench, thinking. I wasn't going to school and knew that would get me into trouble. And that both my parents would be looking for me now and out of their minds with worry. I know this sounds terrible, but even that wasn't important. Parents, school or anything, all I could think about was the puzzle of Deepwater and that horrible phantom thing that attacked me – might still be attacking me in the NUN chamber. I had nowhere to go for the answers and only one place for questions. The institute and that tricky Ms Chibbi Orduna.

I parked my bike by the entrance. The woman at the desk

cleared her throat and started 'little girl'ing but I kept going, on principle. Nobody who calls me little gets an answer.

It was lunch-time again. Chibbi was in her lab, seated cross-legged on one of the long tables, eating riceballs with chopsticks. She looked at me, a riceball between her chopsticks, and shook her head.

'*¿Chica, te has metido en un buen lio?*'

How much trouble could one girl get into? Yes, good question, Ms Tricky, if only you knew. I was in no mood to remember my Spanish.

'Why, am I in trouble with you?'

'With just about everyone but.' She waggled her chopsticks at me. 'Your parents and your teacher have called and want to be told if you show your face. I'd shoot off home if I were you. *Rapido!*'

She held out the carton to me. There was one riceball left and I took it in my fingers.

'How did they know I was here?'

'They phoned everywhere.' A slightly sharper note came into her voice. 'Did you faint again?'

'I was in the park all morning.'

'Not an answer, Denie.' She waggled her chopsticks at me again.

'I'd like to talk to you.'

'And I'd like to talk to you.' She got off the table. 'But not today. *¿Respeta a tus padres?*' I didn't say anything, so she put it into soft English words. 'Honour thy father and mother . . . ?'

'Are you saying I should go home?'

'I'll drive you. And you can come back soon. *¿Hecho?*'

Hecho – yes, it was a deal. No clever questions, no traps, she was so nice under that light teasing voice that my eyes filled with tears.

'Those genes are still OK,' she said.

There was a little question in her voice but I just nodded. She had on a long white blouse with fancy red and blue stitching, a red scarf and chunky silver jewellery. She slipped on her poncho and black leather boots with silver ornaments.

'I'm going dancing tonight,' she grinned and jangled her bracelets, doing a quick two-step in the boots. I just had to smile even though I wanted to burst into tears.

Chibbi talked about the Yucatan on the way home. It is part of Mexico and she has blood of the Mayas, the people who built those huge stone pyramids in the jungle, centuries ago. We stopped at my place and she put her hand on mine.

'We will have that talk,' she said. Her way of saying, Denie, you and I have a secret.

'Promise,' I said. I meant it, I liked Chibbi because she was treating me like an adult.

Then I went inside.

The rest of the day was a total wipe-out. Dad and Mum were home and they were very worried, then a little mad, because I wouldn't give them any answers. Ms Booth came in later that afternoon and told them about the fainting. Her spy system is also grade A. So I told her about Meatgrinder helping me and she nodded like it didn't surprise her.

'Connal is too easily influenced,' she said.

She meant Reeboks, of course. Well, that was her problem. And mine was persuading my parents that I was OK. They got in a doctor to put me through the medical juicer again, but there was nothing wrong. Prexing doesn't show up like a rash or tummy bug. I almost talked them into believing I just fell asleep after all the excitement of turning my enemies into mud pies, but they still landed me with early bedtime.

I couldn't sleep. I have a star pattern of Alpha Centauri pinned to my ceiling and kept looking at it. I even got on a chair and put my finger on it. It was the closest star of all – four and a half years at light speed – but Deepwater was far, far beyond it. Somewhere in the unknown universe I had fought off an alien spacecraft from somewhere else unknown. Then I had been nearly shot into space and a horrible phantom-thing attacked me. Mum chose that moment to come in with cocoa, and I got back into bed quicker than getting shot out of the laser cannon.

She tried to talk to me again. I couldn't talk back, though, as I was afraid it would all come out. Lock it in! When Robbie talked about his prexes to me, it was like a dam bursting. I had a feeling, even then, that my dam should burst in front of Chibbi Orduna.

After the hard, narrow bunks of Deepwater, my bed felt too soft and comfortable. Even the air seemed wrong. This was my third prex and the worst so far. I had felt like a cuckoo on Deepwater, and now I felt like one here.

I got up and pulled on a skivvy and jeans. Then I opened the window and slipped out. It was nearly eleven and both my parents went to bed early. The night was wonderfully cool and I was able to look up at the stars. The Pleiades, the Sisters, Orion and Sirius. Deepwater was far, far past them all, deep in the middle of infinity. And what had that evil thing done to me? Was I back in the casket now? Was I dead? Was it attacking the others? I could feel the evil now, tingling in the cool night air, and I shivered.

There was a clattering sound that seemed to come from the garage. I went round the side of the house. There was light from the street and a skinny figure moving in the shadows. The garage door was open and the little figure was now kneeling just inside. Reeboks – and doing something with my bike!

He looked up. His eyes flashed in the streetlight, then he was up and running across the street. I grabbed a pot of herbs and followed. I was mad, really in the mood to crown Reeboks with the pot.

Reeboks was running down a lane between two houses, moving as fast as a scared rat. I followed and looked round, but he had vanished. Then something moved. I looked up and he was on the roof of a house, sitting astride and looking down at me. How did he get up so quickly? It was like a nightmare.

'Reeboks!' I yelled.

He gave a jeering smile and his teeth flashed in the moonlight. Then someone shouted from one of the houses and a light went on. The flowerpot dropped from my hands with a crash. Goodbye, herbs. I looked back up but Reeboks was gone. Somebody shouted again and I ran back across the street. Luckily no lights were on in my house. I went back into the garage and something else moved in the shadows. I froze.

'Denie?'

I flicked on the garage light. Robbie blinked at me. I looked at him, then reached out quickly and pinched his arm. He yelped. Yes, warm flesh – for a moment I thought it was all a strange dream.

'What'd you do that for?' He nursed his arm. I had pinched very hard.

'Sorry, just checking we were both real.' I was getting tired and hot and felt very unreal. 'What're you doing here?'

He frowned like he was puzzled. 'I . . . I came round, that's all. I think I saw someone.'

There it was in his eyes again, that little flicker of knowing something. He'd come round to see me because a little Reb-spark had told him to look after Denie.

'That was Reeboks. I saw him too, but he got away. He was doing something to my bike, I think.'

Robbie knelt and spun the bike wheel. 'Hey, it's got no brakes.'

I knelt beside him. Our street slopes to the main road and I usually coast down and brake – only this time I would have ended up in a lot of heavy traffic. This feud thing was getting out of hand, but I didn't have time to fight it.

'Robbie, let me handle this,' I muttered.

'Denie, you could have been killed.'

'Please, let me. I can't tell you anything yet.'

60

That little flicker came back into his eyes and I nearly blurted out everything. I turned out the garage light.

'OK, Denie,' he said uncertainly. He had his hand on my arm. It seemed to get very dark, then the lights came back on and he grabbed my arm again. 'You're all right, Denie,' he said again, but I was looking into Reb's face.

I was back on Deepwater. And so quickly this time, my head didn't even spin. I sat up on a bunk, below deck, and Reb gave me some water to drink. Beside him, Bren stood guard, laser rifle in hand.

'That thing—' I shuddered and wanted to be sick. Reb was making me stand.

'A solid-hologram,' he said. 'Didn't quite have the strength to hold itself together.'

'A . . . what . . . ?'

'Explanations in a minute.' Bren was checking the bolt on the airlock door and turned with a grim little smile of sympathy. They'd all prexed, and they knew what it was like coming back. 'Reb, we'd better get on deck.'

'Yes.' Reb's next words sent a big thrill through me. 'Come and have your first real look at Colour-space.'

9   Ambush in Colour-space

A broad, thick stem of bright red waved in the blackness like crimson seaweed. Below was a tangled mass of blue wire drifting in a cloud of yellow and shooting out tiny sparkles of green. In the far distance, a red and purple mass like a nebula seemed to hang in the darkness like a slow-motion explosion.

The ocean floor is black and so is the water. But if all the plant-life was luminous colour, all the unseen fish, currents and even air-bubbles were outlined in glowing patterns of light – that is what Colour-space would look like. It was as though our spaceship was a submarine nosing into the colour-lit blackness of very deep water.

A long way ahead, a diamond rainbow of sparkling dust seemed to stretch from one end of the darkness to the other. Deepwater was keeping well away because trites loved to hide in space dust like that. And we were staying very clear of the drifting colour clouds and gas because a beast of their colours hid among them. Amebs. They were the sharks, and trites were the barracuda of this black-water jungle.

It was beautiful though, incredible, and I was overwhelmed. What causes Colour-space we do not know. Yoona thinks it is a space formation like black holes, a part of the universe breaking down into primary colours – the way clear mist can create a rainbow.

We were holding a council of war on the control deck. Lis was manning the bubble-turret, connected through the intercom. They were all bright kids and knew now what

63

was happening. Why COL was being interfered with, the imitation of Yoona's voice that got me out of Deepwater on to that planet – and the Reb-hologram. They knew who was causing it all.

NUN.

It was a very close escape. Reb had come down a few minutes later to see how I was. I had gone and, with the airlock door still bolted, there was only one place I could be. He called Bren and they had never run down that corridor faster. In the NUN chamber, the almost shapeless Reb-copy was pulling my unconscious body to the far door, that giant, arched slab of rain-crystal that we had never been able to open. One zap from the best laser shot in the universe and it disappeared in a shower of sparkling dots.

'Thanks, Bren,' I said. He just shrugged.

Nobody knew what that thing would have done with me. Nothing nice, that was for sure. NUN had once been all-powerful, controlling their lives, growing from gene cell to childhood. Then it tried to keep them in a golden toyland prison. When they broke free, it tried to get them back and finally they destroyed it.

Or so they had thought.

'We haven't quite destroyed NUN,' said Yoona. 'It's regenerating somehow, getting stronger.' She kept her voice low, uncertain whether NUN could hear her. 'Not strong enough yet to hold its solid-hologram life-forms together for very long, though. They've always been the most difficult.'

'How is NUN moving round?' That was Lis on the intercom. 'Where is it getting an energy source?' There was no answer, for nobody knew.

'And why pick on Denie so much?' said Gret thoughtfully. 'It must hate Yoona and Reb a lot more.'

Yoona thought for a moment. 'Denie got her wake-up after us.' She was steering Deepwater round one of those thick, twisting stems of red. 'It was automatic, controlled by COL.'

'How does that change anything?' said Bren.

'We've all got a programme-memory from NUN except Denie. Maybe NUN doesn't like that, so it's trying to get rid of her first.'

'A cuckoo in the nest?' I said.

Yoona smiled. 'A strong cuckoo.' Deepwater was passing high over the arch of glitter-dust now and it flashed like a giant diamond ring below us. 'You haven't got a programme-memory to fight.'

I thought of that evil hating force in my dreams. None of these kids would let themselves be dominated by NUN again. But a bio-computer, shattered, its programming in pieces, might not be thinking straight any more.

'So NUN has gone crazy,' said Gret. 'How do we stop it?'

'It could be hiding anywhere,' said Bren. He and Gret were scanning ahead because soon we would run into mag-mets, big magnetic meteors that came straight for us. And solunks, which were even worse.

'How do we stop it affecting COL?' came Lis again.

'Ask COL,' I said.

'Now why didn't we think of that?' Bren gave me that big, teasing grin and flipped a dreadlock out of his helmet.

'Maybe you're too busy pulling your hair,' retorted Reb.

That nearly got Bren out of his chair, but Yoona snapped in, just in time. 'Bren, are you checking those mag-mets?'

Her tone made him sit down again. 'Denie, we have asked COL.'

'And COL says no memory,' returned Gret with a green-eyed sour smile at me. 'Yoona, those mag-mets are no problem, they'll pass out of range.'

Yoona nodded, thinking as she watched a long string of yellow circles float past underneath. Overhead, I could hear the bubble-turret tracking round. Everyone was looking around as we spoke, always alert, always poised and ready.

'Then maybe you're not asking the right questions!' I

shouted without meaning to. 'My mum is into computers, and I know you need the right questions for the right answers.'

'Tell us what you mean.' Yoona sounded puzzled.

'COL and NUN are bio-computers, able to regenerate themselves – otherwise they couldn't have lasted so long. Right?' Nobody said anything. Bren rolled his eyes and tugged a dreadlock. They *knew* all this.

'So what's the right question?' said Reb. The arch of glitter-dust was behind now and we were approaching a huge, long cloud of glowing white specks that somehow deflected our scanners.

'Instead of asking it what happened . . .' I was trying to remember what Mum had said about a big computer in America that went funny. ' . . . ask it how it's feeling, like a doctor, where the aches and pains are, you know?' They were all listening now. 'Maybe COL doesn't *know* what's wrong.'

Yoona was looking at me, then ahead. A massive, solid cloud of green gas was building up, like a mountain-sized iceberg. Bren was already scanning and it seemed harmless.

'Tell COL it's sick, then tell it to regenerate?' Yoona smiled, still looking at the green ice-mountain ahead. Then in a very low tone, 'Earthkids are always kicking ass, aren't they Robbie?' They both grinned.

'Blue comet,' said Gret sharply. 'Bearing, variant six.'

'Stations!' yelled Yoona.

Reb slipped into his chair. I turned and clanged in my boots up the spiral stairs to the iron-glass bubble-turret.

'Have a look.' Lis made way for me in the recliner.

Looking into the viewer was like magnifying a wrap-around television screen. When this first happened to Robbie, he had a memory from his programming. I had nothing, so Lis adjusted the vision controls and the picture just zapped out at me.

Swimming up out of that white dot cloud where it had

been hiding – feeding? – came a hosing swirl of deep blue gas. It was flattened at the 'head' like a sting-ray and had a long body-tail that looped back in spirals. It didn't look very big, but was a long way off and we could have flown Deepwater through one of those tail loops.

They had even tried that on the first voyage, Lis whispered, when they were still joy-riding. But those 'comets' have an incredible forcefield that nearly shook Deepwater apart. And although we were thousands of kilometres away, we could feel the forcefield now, tapping against Deepwater's hull like a drumbeat. And there was another very good reason to be careful. Trites hang around inside them for some reason and their first attack had come out of a blue comet. Trites, and COL malfunctioning – that would be real trouble.

The green ice-mountain was looming up on one side of the blackness. On the other side was the comet; we were alongside and running its length. But it was hundreds of kilometres long and the force-vibration tapped on the hull like a horrible giant finger. I began to sense something of the terrible power of deep space. This was getting serious and Yoona had a real problem on her hands.

Yoona had to keep Deepwater between the comet and the ice-mountain. Far enough away from the comet not to be hurt by its power, but not too close to that frozen mass of green. The scans said it was harmless, but in Colour-space you don't take chances.

'This is scary,' I whispered.

'Wait until you see a trite,' said Lis.

She gave me a tight little smile, but I still had the feeling I wasn't accepted. These kids took nothing on trust and everyone had to prove themselves.

'Come down, Denie,' said Yoona in the intercom.

I went back down the spiral stairs. The tapping was louder here, but nobody was taking any chances. There was another sound underneath, a metallic echo.

'What sort of questions should we ask COL?' Her eyes flicked from the comet to the green ice-mountain, keeping Deepwater on the narrowing middle course between them.

I was about to answer when that noise came again. 'I can hear something below deck,' I said. That metallic echo, seeming to mix over the tap-tap of the forcefield.

'Forcefield, that's all.' Yoona was impatient. We had to solve this problem with COL. 'Questions, Denie?'

I could still hear that noise. 'It sounds more than the forcefield,' I said.

'We'll check it out when we're clear of the comet.' Robbie was just as impatient, because the tap-tap of the forcefield was becoming a louder thud-thud-thud.

'We have to take Deepwater right over to the edge of that gas-cloud,' muttered Yoona tensely, 'otherwise the comet's forcefield will start pulling us back.'

'We can't guarantee it's harmless,' said Bren.

'It's green and that's a bad colour out here,' said Reb, adding quickly, 'Nothing personal, Gret.'

She gave him a cold look. 'There are no life scannings.'

'All right,' said Yoona and touched the controls.

She was flying Deepwater by hand, not voice-ac, while COL was still misbehaving. Deepwater moved very close to the gas-cloud and we flew for long, long heart-beats, but nothing happened. The thud-thud became a tap-tap again. And back under it came that metallic echo.

'I can hear that noise again,' I said.

'Trites.'

A single flat word from Lis and did everyone move fast!

'Bearing, Lis,' snapped Yoona.

'Quadrant Four, extreme range twenty, near the comet.'

'COL, vision screen four-twenty.'

The screen flickered up. No sign of trites, just a single broad loop of the comet tail.

'I saw them Yoona, I'm sure I did.'

'Yes, Lis.' Yoona was intent on her console.

68

'Maybe the gas-cloud is screening trites, too,' said Bren.

'Shall I go back up?' I said.

Yoona didn't answer. We were flying so close now that one of the eye-windows was blotted out in bright green. I stood there helplessly and that evil dream-feeling grew on me again.

'Yoona, there's something below.'

'The airlocks are bolted and we're at action stations. Go up to the bubble – now.'

Nobody disobeyed Yoona. Trites had drill-stings that could crack iron-glass. But that feeling of evil grew suddenly worse and I stepped back, clanging my metal boot on the deck button. The hatch slid open.

'Denie!' Reb yelled.

I ignored him – I had to do this. Something was wrong, I knew it.

'Denie, come up and close the hatch,' shouted Yoona in her intercom, very angry.

But I wasn't listening to her. I was chilling with an icy fear and looking at the figure of Reb, standing by the airlock and bashing its hand on the lock bolt. The bolt was nearly clear. It turned to look at me, the eyes glittered and the mouth slipped, seeming to split the face apart in a gaping smile of evil. One more smash of the hologram-hand and the bolt slipped loose.

'Yoona, airlock opening!'

'Close helmets!' she screamed.

The airlock doors were already crashing open and with them, the starboard exit port. A black hole of outer space appeared suddenly at the end of the tunnel and a black solar wind howled through the lower deck. The hologram flickered and blew out like a candle flame. Over that came Lis's louder yell.

'Trites – coming in!'

They saw the open hold and headed straight for it. Yoona put on speed to clear us, but trites go with super-speed. They were headed not for the iron-glass this time, but under the laser cannon straight at the side. Lis got six before they were under her guns and through the port.

I was pulling myself back up in the heavy shoes and helmet. Reb came clanging over, almost in slow motion, to give me a hand. He pulled me through and slammed his gloved hand on the hatch button. Nothing happened. Lis yelled again through her intercom, full of terror.

'More trites – hundreds of them!'

Then with a horrible screeching whirr, like fingernails down a blackboard, the first wave of monster insects screamed through the hatch into the upper deck of Deepwater.

10   Battle inside Deepwater

The last air jet swirled out like water down a plug-hole. The trites spread out, hovering a moment as though surprised to have made it this far. Yoona was rigid at the controls, keeping Deepwater on course. Beside her, Gret and Bren frantically unslung their lasers.

Reb and I rolled over together, our magnetic-soled boots sticking. He was trying to pull me up and unsling his laser rifle at the same time. Our lights were still on, in the dead cold silence of a deep space vacuum. Then the trites swooped and Bren's laser blazed.

Something darkened over my face and I swiped it aside. Now the things were growing wings and eyes out on stalks. Another one zoomed down and beside me, Reb's laser flared, scorching across my face-mask. Bren was guarding Yoona, Gret beside him. Our lasers seared in a deadly flashing criss-cross, but the trites ducked and weaved very quickly and two dived at Robbie and me.

His laser flamed blindingly at one. The other settled on my arm and dug in tiny claws like steel hooks. And that drill-sting grew out of its ribbed underbelly. I was trying to pull it off and Reb smashed it with the butt of his laser.

One landed on Yoona's helmet and Bren shot it off. She was trying to keep Deepwater on an even course. We were at our closest point to the comet and Deepwater was shaking like a rattle. Yoona screamed into the intercom.

'COL, close all the airlocks – close them!'

Then Lis's despairing cry on the intercom, her hatch

71

closed and the boom-boom of the laser cannon overhead. 'Yoona, there are too many, I can't hold them!'

'Tell COL we need it,' I yelled as a trite swooped at Gret and she ducked, laser blazing upward.

Two more trites headed for Yoona. One latched on to Bren, the other on her shoulder. She had to let go of the controls and try to pull it off. Deepwater was drifting now, into the forcefield of the blue comet. The shaking grew stronger. I heard Yoona gasp. Then she spoke – normally, but with an undertone of desperation as she tried to pull the big grey insect off with both hands.

'COL, this is Yoona. We are under attack and you cannot help. You have a virus, fight it – regenerate!' She pulled the trite off, screaming more loudly as another zoomed down. 'You have an enemy – fight it, that is a command!'

The lights dimmed and two of the circling trites collided. Deepwater was shaking from bow to stern. Bren smashed away his own trite and tore Yoona's off as she flung herself on the controls.

'COL, fight it, fight it – that is a command!'

Reb was fighting one. Another zoomed at my face-mask, the drill-sting grew and I remembered the black patch over Gret's eye. I pulled it down, but the trite clung to my arm and I felt a piercing red-hot needle jab. A voice shouted in my intercom.

'Denie, arm up!'

Gret! I raised my arm and she fired from across the deck. The trite shattered into pieces and in the same moment, a loud solid hum of power vibrated through everything.

COL!

It seemed to push back the flickering darkness like a shining sword and that cool-shadow voice sounded strongly through everything.

'Airlock closing.'

The lights came on. Air pressure and Deepwater's returning gravity made our suits and boots heavy. Reb pulled me to my feet, his rifle across us both. Our laser fire had knocked out nearly all the trites, but the airlock closed too late. Another flock of them, more than fifty, zoomed up into the flight deck – too many for our lasers.

Then they swooped, all of them, right at us. Three of them hit me and fell off. The ones still airborne seemed to swerve and hit each other, then crash to the metal floor with a loud rustling sound. COL's deep cool-shadows tones came through this.

'Air pressure restored.'

We raised our visors and looked at the trites in disbelief. What had happened? They moved weakly on the deck, flapping their beetle wings, legs and stings sticking up in the air like spiky thorns, eyes limp on their stalks. One very big one at my feet tried to get up. The goggle eyes grew at me, then it rolled over and down the steps into the lower deck. They were helpless.

Yoona had Deepwater at full power and just in time. The spaceship shook and jarred, but the comet was too far away and slowly we pulled out of the blue coils that would have crushed us. The welcome darkness of deep space closed round and Yoona looked down at the trites, raising her helmet visor.

'Air pressure,' she said.

It was as simple as that. Trites were creatures of outer space, adapted to living in a weightless environment. So air pressure and the artificial gravity that COL created, weighed them down the way a lack of it would make us float. Overhead, the boom-boom of the laser cannon stopped.

'Trites gone, will keep tracking,' came a breathless intercom voice.

The comet was well behind and so was the green ice-mountain. We moved warily, our lasers still ready, in case the trites came back to life. But they just wallowed and flopped like fish out of water. Bren pointed his laser at them.

'No.'

It didn't sound like my voice, even to me. I moved and my arm suddenly hurt sharply. The sight of those things sickened me, but so did the killing.

'Can't we just get them out of the airlock?' My voice trembled because the pain was getting worse.

'They're trites,' said Bren incredulously.

'They can't hurt us now. Trites are like anything, they do what they have to – to survive. What their instincts tell them.'

Gret and Bren were looking at me as though I was crazy. So was Reb, for that matter. But Yoona understood and she nodded. She put out a hand and pushed up the barrel of Bren's laser. 'Just get rid of them.'

Reb nudged Bren. Together, they used their boots and rifle butts to push the clutter of helpless trites down the steps like piles of broken plates. And from there into the airlocks.

My head was spinning and my knees felt rubbery. Someone caught my arm and helped me over to a chair. Gret, her face still white under the green skin, hated and feared trites the way none of us did, but had found time in mid-attack to blast one off me. 'Thanks,' I said, then gasped. Oh, the pain.

'We all know what it's like.' She unclipped a box from beneath her control chair and took out a little thing like a torch battery. 'This'll clean the sting – but it'll hurt.' It did! I gasped more loudly and Gret made to speak, then shut her mouth. She didn't like showing emotion.

Yoona squeezed my hand then, remembering, spoke to the console. 'COL, are your circuits all clear?'

'Yes.'

'COL, can you keep them clear?'

'Yes.'

'COL, is the NUN virus contained?'

'Eliminated.' COL sounded deep, strong and very sure. So we had won the first battle of Colour-space.

'Come on, I'll take you below,' said Gret.

'I'm all right.'

'No, you're not,' she said sharply and Yoona nodded. They didn't need to say I might prex again, as I could see it in their eyes.

Gret helped me to the steps. There were bits of trite and laser scorch-marks everywhere. We went down and over to my bunk as Bren and Reb came back through the airlock.

'Yoona, you can open the starboard exit port,' said Bren. The trites would drop out and Deepwater would be a long way off before they recovered. He went on up and Reb came over.

'I'll sit with you,' he said. NUN was still a menace even though it was out of COL's circuits. Nobody could be left alone.

'I'm doing the first spell,' interrupted Gret in a voice that dared Reb to argue. He looked surprised for a moment, then gave me a quick wink and left. Gret sat down on the next bunk without looking at me again. 'We,' Gret had just said, meaning that even she accepted me now. And not because I'd warned them about those trites – but, I think, because I didn't want them destroyed. They were a strange bunch, but they respected a challenge and I was halfway to understanding them.

The pain in my arm was very sharp and I closed my eyes. In the same half-second, I knew exactly what would happen if I did. My head did that awful inside spin, prexing me across thousands of years in time and space in the blink of an eye. I opened my eyes in darkness, but Deepwater was still so real that my arm ached a moment longer. Then I sat up and turned on my bedside light. I was home again.

There was no more sleep that night. I waited for dawn, the crash and flare of lasers, the screeching trite buzz, going on and on like a video replay in my head.

You would not believe the casual things Mum and Dad swapped over breakfast. About coming home early, meeting

75

cancelled, no appointments after three. In plain talk it meant we want to be with you, Denie – and not let you feel guilty about disrupting our schedules. Then Dad asked me about growing his beard longer and Mum said only if he tied a ribbon in it. As far as parents go, I could have done a lot worse. So I gave them both a big hug before I went out.

I had no bike because of dear little Reeboks, but the rain had stopped so I walked. Robbie pulled up on his bike and got off to walk beside me. He got whistled at by passing kids, but kept walking. He said I'd just gone back into the house last night. He said I'd been 'funny' and he repeated it several times; 'funny', as though it held a memory for him.

He also said I should tell Ms Booth about Reeboks because it was getting serious. I shook my head and he couldn't understand why. Robbie was a nice kid and trying to overcome his male hang-ups about friendship with the other sex. Friendship with the 'sex' removed, if you know what I mean. Boys are always very awkward about that. Today was a half-day and he asked me if I was coming to the hockey match. I smiled, but had to say no. I had other things to do.

Ms Booth was pleased when I told her. 'Yes, something to follow our work on genes. Cloning and how it will change society in the future. Behaviour and instinct too.' She added with a grin, 'That'll give you something to think about.'

It would also let me see a lot of Chibbi without questions being asked. And something she said did get me thinking. Behaviour and instinct. NUN was a very damaged bio-computer and its life spark might be operating on very basic levels. I knew just the guy to ask about animal instinct.

Meatgrinder's dairy and video shop was a very down-market number. Inside it needed a coat of paint worse than Meatgrinder needed a good skin cream for his acne. He was behind the counter already, because Meatgrinder's half-days were always whole ones. He had on a faded red T-shirt with a skull and candle on it, a black 'American Special Forces' baseball cap and a wide leather belt with imitation bullet clips. Round his wrists were spiked leather bands and he was sitting there, pretending to machine-gun passing cars. He scowled, but I wasn't worried. I knew now that a scowl is how Meatgrinder communicates with the human race.

'Geddout,' he snarled, polite as always.

'Does your mum let you turn away paying customers?' I asked and Meatgrinder scowled again. But he changed (tried to short-change) my note into coins. I went over to one of the machines. 'Will you give me a run-through on this?' I asked. It was one of those swords-and-fantasy things with skeletons, chains and monster spiders popping up everywhere.

Meatgrinder scowled knowingly. 'Yeah. Think you can fool me with all this nice-kid stuff?' he sneered. 'Just 'cos you've been overseas and think you're wonderful?' He came over, though.

'I have been like that,' I said. Yes it did sum me up pretty well. 'I've still got a lot to learn.' Being honest got a puzzled scowl from Meatgrinder. 'But it was great the way you looked after me the other day. Now I need your help on something.'

Meatgrinder gave a blank scowl. 'What?'

'If someone was after me, how should I defend myself?'

'Pump-action shotgun.' He was playing the game and he was good. 'There, and you got a free turn, too.' He turned to go and I grabbed his arm.

'Connal!' He got a real shock, I think, as girls do not often lay hands on Meatgrinder. 'How would you deal with a real enemy? What would you do?'

'Geddim first,' he said. 'Leggo.'

I let go. 'What if I didn't know where he lived?'

Meatgrinder gave a frowning scowl and scratched his hands through his black, curly hair. Then he gave a clever scowl. 'Don't have to,' he said. 'Some hit-man wants to blow you away, then he has to find you – geddit? So make him think he's finding you, then geddim. See?'

I did see. Meatgrinder had a really sharp brain when he

tried. And he even forgot to be rude for a minute.

'Thanks, Connal,' I said.

'I'm Meatgrinder!'

'Why?' I had lots of things to do, but I stopped. 'Connal is a great name, it's strong and makes you somebody. Meatgrinder sounds like ground meat – and ground meat is mincemeat.'

Meatgrinder gave an uncertain scowl. 'I'm not mincemeat. What about your game?'

'I'll come back later.'

I turned to go and bumped into Reeboks, creeping up behind. I just kept walking and he yelled as my foot went on his toe – hard. 'I'm sending you the bill for that brake cable and your father will pay if you don't,' I said, wanting to stamp on the other foot.

'What?' Meatgrinder blinked and forgot to scowl.

'And if you're going to involve Connal, tell him first.'

Reeboks was yelling that he hadn't done anything as I walked out. I had borrowed Robbie's bike and checked it for Reeboks-sabotage. Nothing. So I cycled to the institute lab, thinking about what Meatgrinder – Connal – had said. But how could I find out where NUN lived? Deepwater was just too big for the six of us to search it properly. So I had to make NUN come to me – before it made another of those horrible solid-holograms.

It was lunch-time at the institute and there was almost nobody around. I was feeling better, though, and my story pressured inside me to be told. Chibbi would listen, I knew she could.

I went down the corridor into Chibbi's lab. My skin prickled funnily a moment, then I saw her, perched on a lab stool by the long bench. She grinned.

'Hola, chica!'

Just that smile made me feel a lot better. She had on the same blouse and pants as yesterday and the same silver jewellery. And no lab coat.

'Chibbi, can we talk?'

'Sure.' She indicated her big microscope. 'Come and have a look at this first.'

I went over and sat on the lab stool. Chibbi stood behind me. She wasn't wearing that nice jasmine scent. I was about to look in the microscope, then saw something reflected in the window.

There were two Chibbis in the room. The first was standing behind me, the other was in the corner, frozen in the act of putting on her lab coat. That tingling in my body when I came in – same clothes as yesterday, no scent – what a fool I was!

I jerked round. Behind me, the Chibbi-copy was raising a hypodermic needle. Her eyes glittered as she lunged at me and the big smile split her face in half.

11   The creature from NUN

I spun the stool round and threw myself clear. The needle broke on the table beside me. I was already rolling over the floor and heading for the door. I had it open, but the Chibbi-thing moved as quick as a panther. It flung me aside and kicked the door shut, facing me with a huge, horrible grin, the broken hypodermic in its hand.

It took one step forward like the panther getting ready. The mop of black hair shook round glittery eyes. I was picking myself up, looking round for something to defend myself with. There was nothing but Chibbi's big, black, silver-banded hat on another labstool. Then the Chibbi-thing sprang, face gleaming and the needle raised. I whipped up the hat and skimmed it at her like a black saucer.

It hit her and the silver band flashed. The Chibbi-thing flickered and collapsed in a shower of dots, vanishing, seeming to suck into an opening slit behind her like dirt into a vacuum cleaner. Everything disappeared and I collapsed on the floor.

'Denie!'

The real Chibbi was pulling me up. I hugged her, smelling the jasmine. I should have guessed the moment I was in the lab, for nobody wears the same clothes after a night's dancing.

'¿Qué te pasa, Chica?'

A hell of a lot is the matter, Chibbi. I was pale and breathless and I couldn't speak. She got me a glass of water, then saw the broken hypodermic and picked it up. She sniffed what was inside it and went as pale as me. Then she emptied it and washed her hands very carefully.

'Where did you get that?' No more Spanish, no more jokes.

'Do you really want me to tell you?'

'Bet your life, kid.'

'All right. After our talk yesterday, I prexed again. Somehow a bio-computer that hates me managed to screen my mind and pick up my last image of you. Then it made a copy, a solid-hologram, and sent it here into my prex. Time stopped for you while it was here. It somehow got that hypodermic and drugs and waited for me. Maybe if it killed me here, then I'd never wake up on Deepwater.'

I tried to keep my voice level, but I felt cold and shivery and kept sipping the water. Chibbi refilled the glass.

'And where is it now?' she said, also in a very level voice.

'It disappeared when I threw your hat at it. I think the silver made it short-circuit.'

She didn't phone for the doctor or anything like that. She made me repeat the story, then she checked for her keys. They were missing. She found them in the drugs cabinet door and a plastic bottle of something had been opened.

'I've been in the lab since I came in,' she said. 'I haven't opened that cabinet and nobody could do it without me knowing.'

'I told you, time stopped,' I said.

Chibbi didn't want to believe me at all. She even shook her head, but she was shivering a little like me. 'My mother's blood,' she said, half to herself. 'Something evil has been here, I can sense it. I want to hear all of it, Denie.'

I was ready, but she wasn't. She locked the lab door, pulled down the blinds and took the phone off the hook. Then she made us both coffee. She kept giving me dark, serious looks, but she was very calm.

'You don't seem bothered,' I said.

'Denie, I'm very bothered.' Her cup clattered on the table a moment. 'And I'm ready.'

A journalist, even a wannabe like me, should be able to tell a story properly. But I didn't have to try – it was like switching on a tape-recorder inside me. I just started talking and didn't stop for a long time.

I began from that first day in class when Robbie prexed. The sun was streaming in the window and there were traffic sounds in the distance. I talked about black space and Colourspace, NUN and COL and kids, red, blue, brown and green. About a living planet with green-blue trees and black snake-ships. Footsteps went up and down the corridor outside, once with loud voices, and somebody knocked on the lab door a moment. I just kept talking about trites and amebs, blue comets and green icebergs, the Earth colonies on Mars and the little upper cabin on Deepwater where the bodies of the first crew lay. Mostly I talked about the five other kids who needed me right now . . . who were somewhere in the universe, fighting the last battle of the human race.

When I finished, the sun was making dark square blocks of afternoon shadow. Chibbi hadn't touched her coffee. Then she began asking questions, sharp and tricky and some were meant to trap me. She shot them so quick I felt like a trite dodging bolts from the laser cannon. Her brown eyes stayed on me like searchlights.

Then she slipped off her stool and began walking up and down the room. Today she had on a blue and red polka-dot blouse, a beaded waistcoat and a long yellow skirt. She walked up and down for a few minutes and once she stopped by the drugs cabinet and jiggled her keys.

Then she sat down again, leaning her elbows on her knees and with her chin cupped in her hands.

'Do you believe me?' I said.

'You believe it,' she said, looking at me.

'That's not an answer, Chibbi.'

'I went through some kind of blackout. As a scientist, that's all I know.'

'And you felt that evil?'

'I felt something.' But she moved a bit like the memory made her uneasy.

'Do you believe enough to keep those genes safe?'

'Yes.' I think she did, then she gave a little confused headshake and said abruptly, 'When do you think you'll prex again?'

It was strange listening to her use that word. She said it in such a matter-of-fact scientific way that I nearly felt uneasy. Deepwater wasn't private to me any more; Chibbi was going to put it under her microscope.

'Denie, do you feel threatened?' She had an uncanny way of reading minds.

'A little. Will you help?'

She gave me a wonderful big smile. 'Sure.'

It was such a good feeling I nearly burst into tears and hugged her really tight. She laughed, but it had a little choke to it and she hugged me back even tighter.

'All my scientific training says this is in your mind, Denie.'

'What does you mother's blood tell you?'

'Chica, it tells me you might be in real danger.' She went very serious. 'Don't look evil in the face because it might take your soul.'

'I'll be careful.'

'You be more than careful.' She thought for a moment, running her hands through her hair the way Yoona did. 'I have to finish a few things, make some phone calls. Then I'll take you home.'

'Thanks.'

Chibbi was looking at me like she'd remembered something. 'Did you say my hat made that thing short-circuit?'

'I think the silver did.'

She picked it up and ran her finger round the band. It comprised big discs with a spiral pattern and each had a little blue stone set in the middle. 'Silver is supposed to destroy evil.'

'That's horror film rubbish,' I said. Did she think I was getting all this from a B grade video?

'Or maybe the metal had a disrupting influence on that light-force.' She gave another little shiver like her mother's blood was telling her something. 'You hang on to my hat.'

It was a great hat! 'I can't take this.'

'You keep it.' She gave me a little push towards a chair by the window. 'Now sit down, I won't be too long.'

'Thank you, Chibbi.'

She smiled again and gave another of those little headshakes like she couldn't understand what she was doing. I sat down in the chair, thinking about those black metal chairs on the control deck of Deepwater. Were the trites attacking again while I was lost in my prex? It was raining now, and water was running down the windows. Chibbi tipped her hat over my eyes.

'Relax,' she said. '*Echa una cobezadita.*'

I did feel like a little sleep and she turned back to the lab bench. The hat smelled good, like her, and I smiled at the thought of showing it to Mum and Dad – but neither of them was going to wear it. Then I thought of something else and spoke into the hat as I closed my eyes.

'We have to keep this between ourselves, Chibbi.'

'Who's Chibbi?' said Yoona.

I was back on Deepwater, on my bunk. Yoona was with me; they'd all taken it in turns in case NUN reappeared. I felt heavy and empty, but wide awake.

'Where are we?'

'Still in Colour-space,' said Yoona. 'Co-ordinates for the other Deepwater are close to matching.'

Gret and Lis were asleep on the other bunks. I told Yoona

what had happened. She had taken off her space suit and sat, elbows on knees, her chin cupped in hands, the way Chibbi did. When I got to the part about the Chibbi-copy, she gasped and pulled her hands hard through her blonde and red hair.

'We were with you all the time. How did NUN get into your prex?'

'I don't know.' I was remembering, though, that prickly feeling on my body. I'd felt it the time I chased Reeboks too. How could a kid have jumped so quickly on to the roof of a house? That must have been a NUN creature too! Yoona heard it all, then began walking up and down, thinking. We talked in whispers so as not to wake the others.

'The lights were on all the time. Nothing came near you.'

'All the time – nothing happened?'

Yoona shrugged. 'They dimmed a little once or twice.'

Oh, that had to be it. 'Yoona, they flickered the time I heard your voice.' Now it zapped through me like a laser-flash. 'And when I saw that Reb-thing . . . !'

'Transmission of energy.' Yoona stopped pacing. 'Lights, the light circuits, *that's* how NUN is moving – getting its energy.' Then she sank on a bunk despairingly. 'But we must have thousands of them in Deepwater, we'd never know where to look.'

'He has to look for you – geddit?' I could almost hear Meatgrinder speaking those words in my head. NUN was looking for me, we didn't have to look for NUN. Yoona made me eat a biscuit and drink some water. Then I spent ten wet and dry seconds in the shower-lick. She was shaking Lis awake when I came out.

'Relieve Bren in the bubble,' said Yoona. She lay down, closed her eyes and was asleep at once.

'And remember, it's *my* bubble,' grinned Lis cheerfully.

On the control deck, Reb was steering Deepwater alone. His silver-grey track suit was stained and torn. There were others in the store lockers but they always wore the same one, cleaning it and themselves in the shower-lick. It was a point of pride, like having the same old faded denims. Mine were still new and looked much too clean and respectable.

I told Reb about NUN and the prex. It was great watching him at the steering console of a giant spaceship. The more so because part of him was still my Earth-Robbie, whose biggest problem two weeks ago was getting his homework in on time. He took Deepwater up and over a long luminous purple strand in the blackness.

'NUN could be hiding anywhere. There are parts of Deepwater we've never been into.' He spoke into the console. 'COL, give us the location of your power source and master terminal.'

'Information withheld.'

'NUN must be somewhere. We could set a trap—'

'Don't even think about it,' snapped Reb. 'We have to get to the other Deepwater first. And we wouldn't know where to look – Yoona's right.'

I got up to go but paused a minute, looking into the blackness ahead. I didn't think NUN would wait for us. It wanted me more than any of the others and would come searching for me again. I went up the stairs to the bubble, thinking about it, but knowing already what I had to do. I had to let NUN find me before it wrecked the spaceship.

And that was a meeting only one of us would walk away from.

12 Hide and seek with something evil

'Reb, I have that mag-met on screen now.'

Bren had scarcely spoken to me since I got into the recliner beside him. He was focusing on a magnetic meteor coming towards Deepwater and I clicked on my side of the screen. There it was, a rolling ball of jagged, grey rock. Magnetic meteors could not be avoided and had to be destroyed. Bren was already locking the sights of his laser across it.

'Ready when you are, Bren,' came Robbie's voice.

The recliner jarred as Bren fired the laser cannon. A yellow fire-needle hit the mag-met dead centre and exploded it into fragments. Bren grinned and drank out of a squeeze-bottle. He didn't say anything, but that was OK with me because I just wanted to sit there and take in the wonder of being on top of Deepwater, with the upended black bowl of Colour-space round us, so incredible and huge that it made our giant spaceship seem like a speck of cosmic dust. Over to one side was a gas formation like knotted lumps of pale red ribbon and far behind, a row of six square beads. Bren pointed at it and spoke casually.

'Ameb.'

Ameb! I nearly jumped because they'd all told me how terrible amebs were. A sort of monster jellyfish-octopus, almost impossible to kill and able to make itself look any innocent colour or shape. The big ones could crush Deepwater easily. Bren was watching me, maybe hoping I would freak.

'Are we going to invite it in for dinner?' I said.

Bren just grinned. The ameb was closer now and looked like a piece of thickly-knotted rope. But it was only a small one. Bren read off the closing distance into the intercom and our vision screen angled as Robbie moved Deepwater slightly. Then he fed a charge of extra energy into the engines and it shot out of the exhaust like an invisible bullet of unburned energy. It caught the ameb dead-centre and split it into pieces, like a jelly hit by a guided missile. We would be many thousands of kilometres away by the time it reformed.

It was good for me, sitting up in the bubble. I could realise now what they were all going through. There were sudden sharp moments of desperate action, but most of the time it was like this, being tired, trying to stay alert and fighting sleep, letting all black space go by. My back ached and so did my wrists, but I made myself lie there, alert and always watching. This was the real life of Deepwater that Bren and the others lived all the time. No videos, parties, music, new clothes or fun. Just work and sleep and always waiting for danger that might kill them all. They had been through it once and now they were doing it again.

'What's it like on Planet Earth?' said Bren suddenly.

I tried to tell him about the green fields, the blue sky and water, because those were the images that came. I also tried to tell him how we were cleaning up the planet but it sounded too silly – because we didn't do enough in time, and that was why Deepwater was launched. So I asked him what life was like on the solar colonies.

'You'd know that if your programme-memories had worked, Cei.' He used the name on my tunic. 'You're a colour-freakie like us.'

Us? Then I clicked. He was talking about my brown-red skin and red hair. Robbie had told me about the different ozone-layers and sun-filters; colonists on North Mars and the asteroid mining bases were green, blue and red. Like Gret, Lis and Bren.

'Earth would have called you a freakie. Or a tint, rock-head, sandbrain. We were good enough to keep the minerals coming, but we stuck out like sore thumbs on Earth. Coloured thumbs, red, blue and green,' Bren said.

'But the South Martians were the same.' Wrong thing to say!

'Puddle-bunnies!' Bren was using a very rude personal Martian nickname. 'A nice respectable golden-brown, all very hi-tech.' He laughed. 'They melted the icecaps to terraform Mars and turned the Hellas basin into a swamp.'

'Those are just programme-memories. Why do they matter here?'

'They matter,' said Bren, and didn't speak again until Lis came up to relieve us.

'Get out of my bubble,' she said, grinning. One blue-skinned arm was bare because her track suit had a sleeve missing, stripped away in a fight with jel. She could handle the turret on her own.

Yoona was on deck, taking Deepwater up, up, over a big glinting mass of red-yellow, shot through with flashes of orange like strobe lightning. The huge spaceship responded like a tame puppy.

'Get some sleep, you two. I make the wreck about three hours ahead if I time-blink. We'll need everyone then.'

'Are we in that much of a hurry?' said Bren.

'Yes.' Yoona was still watching the red-yellow mass as it fell behind. 'Deepwater was built for one interstellar voyage, not two.'

Reb was already asleep when we went down. Bren was supposed to sit up, but he was so tired he began to doze straight away and I let him. I sat up on my bunk, waiting for the lights to dim. Thinking about NUN, unseen and horrible, sending its energy awareness creeping silently through the lighting circuits. I let my mind go as blank as I could and waited, feeling like bait on the end of a hook.

Overhead, the lights dimmed a moment. NUN was here.

Reb and Bren were sound asleep and I was careful not to disturb them as I stood. I could feel NUN, scanning me like a current of cold water running over my brain and through my body. I began to feel very afraid, but calm. The others were running Deepwater while I prexed, so now it was time for me to do something. Something they couldn't.

Find NUN.

The lights dimmed again as though NUN was saying yes, try and find me. Our palm-prints opened the lock, Reb had told me that. I was back in that long, metal corridor that led to the NUN chamber. I shut the door and began to walk down.

Denie, you don't really know why you are doing this, I said to myself, but kept walking. Light came from the interlocking circles overhead, but the corridor was silent. My skin began to prickle as it did when I met that Chibbi-thing. Nothing else happened, but I knew something was scanning me.

I went through the other door into the NUN chamber. The other door closed behind me with that unpleasant coffin-shutting sound. I stood in those cold, metal shadows and *felt it* as, from the overhead darkness, something opened a malignant eye. Malignant as in wishing evil, harmful and likely to cause death. Yes, this eye wished to cause my death and my skin was prickling hard.

I kept walking, past the rain-crystal caskets now and trying to remember what Chibbi had said – don't look evil in the face. There was still nothing but the cold, bare metal shadows and the evil, unseen, watching thing.

'NUN!' I shouted. My voice raised a hundred ghostly echoes laughing back and that malignant presence seemed right overhead. 'NUN – if you want me, here I am!'

'Am . . . am . . . am . . .' The ghosts had a good laugh at that one, too.

'I know you are listening!'

There was no answer. But now a very slight noise like

huge shuffling feet was making its own echo. I turned round.

At the other end of the NUN chamber was the NUN door. It was six metres high, shaped to a point and made out of solid rain-crystal. Once, a golden light had shone from behind that door because it led into the bio-terminal heart of NUN itself. As I watched, the shuffling noise began again, coming from the door as it moved – the door that none of us had ever seen open.

But it was opening now.

Suddenly I was very scared. What had I done? I was here, in the middle of Deepwater, alone and facing a terrible enemy . . . not knowing how strong it was, how it would attack me. I'd wanted to do this alone and now I was alone. So I had to go on.

The rain-crystal door was fully open now showing an arched, black entrance. Above, the presence looked at me from flickering shadows as I walked up. The entrance's blackness lightened a little because NUN wanted me to see where I was going. I walked inside and with a horrible quick thud, like a tiger pouncing, the door slammed shut.

The room inside arched to a higher point than the door. It still flashed yellow in parts and was set with overlapping layers of crystals, bigger than any I had seen. They were dark and I touched one. It fell to powder. The floor was ankle-deep with a thick red dust. NUN had once had a bio-mass regenerating body. Maybe the dust was all that remained. I touched another crystal and it crumbled. But I felt NUN's presence in this dark place and I kept walking.

Ahead was a blank wall, like rain-crystal but different. I put my hands on to it and they pressed in. I took a deep breath and walked straight into the wall. It folded round me like cool, soft ice – a force-wall, becoming solid on the other side.

This room had a curved roof and a floor that was black and shiny, like plastic. I had never seen a black floor anywhere else on Deepwater and I went to my knees a moment, pressing hard. I thought of Chibbi for some reason. I had an incredible feeling that under this black floor lay the greatest secret of Deepwater. But the lights were flickering, so NUN was watching. I walked on and into the next wall. Another forcefield, and going solid behind me. It was one-way, so now two force-walls and a sealed door shut me off from the rest of Deepwater. NUN was leading me forward into its trap.

Ahead was an empty, twisting, almost round passage-way. The walls were studded with thousands of tiny holes. I had to look, think and remember. This must be the gene bank Robbie had talked about. Once a light river had flowed here and each hole held a gleaming diamond-like crystalloid, enclosing a life form. Now the passage was still, the light river gone, the holes empty and everything dry of life.

Onward, Denie, come to me, said that voice, still malignant but now with a sense of something else.

I was feeling sick and dizzy – not a prexing dizziness, just fear, knowing all of this was too much. I was too alone and all too aware of how powerful NUN was; it was getting stronger as it sucked energy from our light circuits.

I walked down the long, twisting corridor. The gene bank that had slept here all those centuries was now back on Earth and we had to find another Deepwater – with another gene bank.

I was at a round airlock door now. It led through to the exhaust chambers that vented the waste gas from Deepwater's engines out into deep space. I pushed through the door into the first chamber. It clicked shut behind me and a blue-white bar of light came blindingly down. Reb and Yoona had told me about those – sealing lights to destroy anything alien entering the ship.

There was an airlock hatch set in the ceiling. Reb had told me about that, too. I pushed it open and climbed through. It clicked shut behind me and lights came on. They flickered and I felt that little tingle of something evil watching. A metal ladder led up into the blackness and I hesitated. Everything was cold and silent. I thought of Chibbi again and that wonderful black hat of hers. I could even hear her voice . . . you have to do this, Denie, but don't look evil in the face.

I began to climb.

The ladder seemed to stretch up forever. It must have been a hundred metres high. I dared not look down at the darkness and once my gloved hands slid on the railings. I reached the top and scrambled on to a metal walkway that stretched ahead like the metal spine of this deep space whale.

Come, Denie . . . but hesitating. Didn't NUN think I would get this far?

I began to walk. This was the last section of Deepwater to be built. On the walls and overhead were little scratched messages from the colonists on Mars who had stripped their cities and given up their own chances of life to build the two Deepwaters. Dying of a space virus, with Planet Earth already dead, they were working to give human and animal life another chance.

It seemed to go on forever. The lights were coming on at intervals, then going off behind me. The darkness opened ahead and closed behind, making me move. Then one light showed a sudden glimmer of pale movement and I stopped, screaming inside. A figure stepped into the light.

Yoona.

Her face was pale and she was breathless. She must have gone through the old control room ahead that Deepwater's first crew used when they took off from Mars in 2090. All that was left of them was still there.

'Denie – where've you been?'

'Yoona's taken her space suit off, NUN.' I couldn't believe how calm I sounded. 'You're not scanning very well.'

Yoona looked at me, then her face and body twisted somehow and she vanished. I felt even better. NUN was

95

ahead and trying to stop me – because for some reason it was afraid.

The control room door now.

I stopped and breathed deeply, putting myself into shut-down mode for a moment. Little sparks of panic came through and I tried to imagine Chibbi's big black hat on my head. I breathed in that warm good-person smell of hers and felt the warmth flow in, telling me not to be scared – you can handle this, Denie.

And Denie, said the soft Chibbi-voice, remember . . . don't look evil in the face.

All right Chibbi. Thank you. Here goes.

I opened the door. The old control room was nearly black, but some lighting flickered on. The 'ceiling' was the silver-plate outer skin of Deepwater itself. More light, enough to push the darkness into blue-black puddles and show four control chairs. Four empty space suits and helmets were collapsed on them in a shapeless seated position. The humans in those suits had long ago turned to dust. KANER and ERL. The two far ones were BARLA and TEM – Yoona's parents.

'NUN . . . ?'

Something seemed to scuttle like a spider and I tensed. The darkness moved a little and the lights flickered. I was cold, breathing in thick dust that made me sick. I could feel that little panic spark again and spoke more loudly.

'NUN!'

There was nothing but that little spider shuffling again.

'NUN – why me? Why do I scare you so much?'

That spider shuffling sound came again and I saw movement by one of the chairs. A boot was scraping on the floor, then one of the crumpled space suits shifted slightly. It was moving.

Gloved empty hands clutched slowly at the arm-rests and the boots moved again. Fighting the mad desire to run, I stepped quickly, wanting to scream as the crumpled figure rose to its feet. Kaner's space suit was sagging like an empty puppet, the helmeted head nodding as though about to fall off. I could sense little vibes of fear from it.

'They made you too well, NUN.' I wanted to choke and scream at the same time. 'I know you're trying to regenerate your bio-mass. How does killing me help?'

'Denie . . .' whispered a dry croaking voice inside the helmet.

A limp gloved hand was moving slowly up. Then those little fear vibes I had been getting from NUN somehow stopped. And suddenly I understood, everything, how NUN had tricked me! Not scared, it wanted to trap me – it wanted my life-force for its bio-mass! It all came through in Chibbi's voice, screaming that same loud warning in my head.

Don't look evil in the face!

The gloved hand flicked up the helmet visor. I squeezed my eyes shut but the sharp, burning pain went through my eyelids and into my head. I threw myself back, the helmet visor snapped down again and the space suit thing lunged at me.

13   The electronic vampire strikes

There was a door behind and another stairway leading down
to the airlock passage. I jerked it open as a gloved hand
caught my wrist. Empty steel fingers closed in a tight grip
and I tore free as a burning pain seared my wrist. I flung
myself down the stairs and the thing followed – the newest
crew-member full of the fresh energy that NUN needed, like
a vampire seeking blood.

I ran madly down more stairs, the space suit thing
clanging after me like a horrible full-size doll, one hand
out. I was quick, leaping several stairs at a time because all
the thing had to do was fall on me. It would never let go, it
would suck out my life-force like a draining battery. I had
one chance only at the bottom of the stairs, over the airlock
passage.

The bottom hatch was ahead. Even in the space suit and
heavy boots, the NUN thing moved with hideous speed. It
was only a clang-step behind as I pulled the hatch open.
The cold, burning glove-hands grabbed for my face as I dived
through, NUN falling on top of me. This *had* to work or I
was dead!

But I knew something NUN didn't. At least I was hoping
it didn't. NUN was a bio-computer, but only COL controlled
the operation systems of the ship. And over this airlock
passage was another of those solid light bars to stop anything
alien passing to or from the top of Deepwater via the airlock
passage.

The blue-white light bar passed over me like a solid blade,

without hurting. Anything human could get through, but NUN was not human. It was pulled after me and as it was, the light bar scorched and crumpled the suit, squeezing it flat. There was a high, furious screaming sound – not just of something dying, but of something being destroyed and knowing it was finished.

The space suit crumpled over me and the hatch clicked shut overhead. I pulled the empty gloves from my wrists and the helmet rolled away, empty. I am glad I never saw the face.

The airlock hissed open and Reb was there with Bren. I scrambled up, pointing to the crumpled suit.

'NUN.'

Reb pulled me through and hit the airlock button. It slid shut again and they pulled me over to a bunk. The scream of NUN's destruction had rung through all Deepwater.

'Come up!' shouted Yoona on the intercom and they helped me to the upper deck. They listened in silence as I told them what had happened. I was shaking and my knees had that horrible wobbly feeling again. Then Yoona gave a set of orders to COL and the airlocks hissed open and shut. The empty space suit and helmet were air-blasted out into deep space and with them, we hoped, whatever remained of the burned-out life force of NUN. Then she gave me one of her looks. Here it came!

'Denie—'

'I had to do it!' I yelled. 'That thing was after me – nobody else could have found it. OK, it was wrong and NUN nearly got me, but I had to make myself useful.' My hands were burning like fire and I looked down. Round each wrist were black marks like glove prints and I wanted to burst into tears. 'All right,' I was still yelling, 'I'll go back to my casket now and sleep-dream as Denie Miles and you won't have to worry about me or NUN!'

'You're not Cei—' began Yoona but I interrupted.

'No! I can't be her, I'm an Earthkid, I *think* like one and

I always will, so you'd better finish this voyage without me.'
I turned and headed for the hatch. Yoona's voice stopped
me.

'Welcome aboard, Denie Miles.'

Reb was gently pulling me back. Gret pulled out her
medical kit and pressed a little sonic thing on my wrist marks
that eased the pain. Bren gave me a squeeze-bottle and
growled, 'Denie the NUN killer,' before going back below.
Reb just winked and followed him. I felt truly, one hundred
per cent, accepted, and wished the silly tears would stop
falling down my cheeks. Lis came racing down for a quick
hug and the tears got even worse. Gret nudged me into Reb's
chair and, after a few minutes, the stupid things dried up.

Yoona was flying Deepwater through all this, without
looking at me. There was a jumble of yellow and purple
nearby like ragged curtains and it looked so innocent that
she was giving it as wide a berth as possible. Far below was
one of those long cloud reefs, this one was dark yellow and
lit with strobe lightning. Yoona waited until she was well
clear, then did a wonderful thing. She reached over, took
my hand and pressed it on the crystal console before her.

'COL, Denie is sharing voice-ac, respond please.'

'Confirmed.'

They had all done this at one time or another. Everyone
had to know how to fly Deepwater. But that hundred-per-
cent feeling doubled inside me because in a complete
unspoken way, Yoona was saying thank you for saving us.
And welcome aboard, Denie Miles, said her big, lovely smile
again.

Yoona and Gret showed me how to use the scanners. It
wasn't difficult, as the hologram readouts picked up most
hazards and we could alter course to avoid them. My big
moment came when we detected some big meteors like steel-
blue bowling balls. I spoke the course alteration and thrilled
as Deepwater at once altered course. Soon the meteors were
tumbling past and overhead, Lis tracked the laser cannon

on them in case trites were hitching a ride. Then Yoona took full voice-ac back, but I couldn't resist putting my hand on the console just once more.

'COL, thanks for zapping NUN like that.'

The console glowed a sudden deep crimson and I felt a little charge of power go through me. 'COL must like you,' said Yoona. 'How did you know it *would* zap NUN?'

'I just felt it,' I said. She was about to say something else then Gret's voice cut sharply across.

'Solunk!'

Yoona took Deepwater sharply starboard. Gret pointed, but it was some time before I saw it. A blacker mass among the black, shining oddly at the edges. Solid chunks of solar nothing, the kids nicknamed them, but they had their own forcefields and were very dangerous. The big ones were like super-huge icebergs and sometimes had to be rammed.

'We haven't seen many this trip,' said Yoona as she settled Deepwater back on course. She looked up at some white light flicking overhead like arrows. 'We have the settings and we're on a more direct course.'

My wrists still hurt, so Yoona and Gret kept talking. It was their way of helping me to take my mind off the pain – and letting the horrible memories of that NUN thing begin to fade. The solunk was a glimmering patch of total black, far behind us. I began thinking about that other Deepwater.

'How far ahead can we scan?' I asked.

'Not far enough for the other Deepwater.' Once again, Yoona had tuned uncannily to my thoughts. 'But I can show you the vision log from our first voyage.' She flicked a crystal for the coordinates. 'COL, vision log, c.c. 165-1944.' Numbers flicked on the big overhead screen then it snapped into life, showing a picture so terrible that I forgot the pain in my wrists.

Another Deepwater, wrecked and torn apart, lay before us. The structure held together, but was bent and twisted out of shape. The cabin area was shattered, the eye-windows black and sightless. The giant exhaust housings had torn loose and all the silver-plate scales had peeled off. The difference between this and our Deepwater was like contrasting a living streamlined fish with a skeleton backbone and skull, in a puddle of its own shed scales.

None of us could bear the sight of it for very long. Yoona took it off the screen. 'One more gulf coming up. If it's clear then, we'll time-blink.' Her voice was sad with painful memories. 'Then we'll be there.'

'And hope we find some of the gene bank,' Gret said softly.

None of us wanted to think about that. COL had said the genes would survive as units – but the hundred dangers of Colour-space would not have left them alone.

'How will you get inside that?' I couldn't call it a Deepwater.

'OMA.' Yoona did not have to add that she would be piloting it.

I dropped my voice to a whisper. 'Can I go with you?'

'Why?'

'I just have a feeling I should.' I did too, it was like something glowing inside me. Then, just as I said that, COL's console glowed a moment as well, a deep sudden pulse of red. Gret did not see it, only Yoona and I. It was as though COL was saying something, giving approval. Yoona did not reply, but gave me one of her deep, golden-brown looks.

'COL really does like you,' she said softly.

That was all she said. I lay back in the chair and shut my eyes a moment. I must have slept because when I woke, Bren and Reb were up on deck, standing beside us. And I blinked because ahead, through the eye-windows, was the same picture of the wrecked spaceship that I'd seen on screen from the vision journal. Only this one was real. The other Deepwater in deep space was before us.

* * *

'We don't know if those gene crystals will register,' said Reb. He was back in his chair and we were circling the dead-looking, smashed thing that had once been a spaceship. 'Anyway, the hull would block most of our scan.'

Nobody spoke. We all knew that we had to check inside. The glass bubble-turret had torn itself loose and was floating nearby, upended like a smashed glass egg. Lis's voice came suddenly, from our turret.

'Yoona, focus on the starboard exit port, I can see something.' Her cannons trained to cover it as she spoke.

Yoona gave COL the readings and the curved vision screen sprang into 3-D life again. The exit port was open and black, and round it seemed to be clusters of tiny round balls.

'What are *those?*' said Reb.

Yoona spoke to COL again and there was utter silence as she focused them up in a magnified box. Then she magnified further, closing in on one of the balls. It was pitted and rough, a dark grey colour. Bren gave a relieved sigh.

'Meteorite. A small one.'

'They're all meteorites?' Reb wasn't convinced.

Yoona zapped the box all over the exit, focusing on one, then another. There were about fifty of them, all about the same size and colour, in groups and on their own.

'Little mag-mets, stuck to each other?' came Lis on the intercom.

'Maybe.' Yoona wasn't certain either. In Colour-space you don't take chances. Our scanners showed no life-readings, but they didn't always pick everything up. None of us really thought those things were meteors. We didn't know what they were.

'OMA or a Wingfish?' said Reb.

'OMA first. I want to see what's there before we take in anything bigger.'

'Yoona, I'll go with you,' came Lis's voice at once.

'It's my job!' shouted Reb.

'Who the hell decided that?' growled Bren.

'Yes, you smashed one of our OMAs,' snapped Gret.

'Shut up all of you!' shouted Yoona, as though keeping order in the classroom. 'I'm going and taking . . .'

'Me?' I was taking a chance interrupting, but had my arguments all set. 'I've been through all of Deepwater, even the crystal door. I know the layout.' Nobody spoke. 'And that'll still leave a full working crew behind and . . .'

'I've already decided,' interrupted Yoona back again. 'And I'm taking . . .' stopping long enough to make me squirm ' . . . you'.

'Yoona . . .' Reb stopped as I dug him in the ribs.

'Thanks, Yoona.' I was heading downstairs before anyone could ask 'what if she prexes?' and was halfway into my space suit when Yoona came down.

'Denie, this is going to be very dangerous.'

'I want to do it.'

She just nodded and began putting on her space suit. It did make sense to take me, but as commander she still had to make the decision. Then Bren came down and went through the airlocks to the main port. Yoona and I put on our helmets, slung on our laser rifles and followed. Bren already had the OMA out. His brown-red face was set and tight but he tried to grin.

'Careful of those space rock things. They might be junior amebs.' He made to go back through the airlock. 'We will find something, won't we, Yoona?' She just nodded and the airlock shut. They don't come any tougher than Jupie rockheads, but even Bren was ready to come apart over this one.

Nobody else said anything through the intercom. This was something that words just could not convey. Yoona whispered a 'good luck' to me as she sealed her helmet visor and I whispered one back, before sealing mine. We could hear Robbie instructing COL, then the exit port rolled sideways and Yoona took the OMA through. It was all happening very quickly because none of us wanted to wait or think about it. I glimpsed the silver-plate sides of Deepwater stretching out, but didn't look back. Leaving the spaceship scared me, but I was even more scared of what lay ahead.

All too soon we would know if the human race was finished.

14 Ghost lights

It would take long minutes to cross this black ocean of nowhere to the other ship and Yoona didn't waste any time. She set the controls and we both kept our laser rifles ready. The OMA cockpit covers would not keep out trites very long, so it felt good to know that Lis was sitting behind the cannons back on Deepwater. Slowly, the wrecked spaceship grew larger before us. It must have been worse for Yoona. She had seen this Deepwater when it was still whole.

'Tell me what happened . . . please?' I only knew a little, because even Reb didn't like talking about it.

Yoona breathed heavily as though getting something bad-tasting out of her mouth. 'We found it by accident. Undamaged, just like our own ship. Reb and I went across in an OMA. The airlocks were open, but there was nobody on the decks. So we went through to the NUN chamber.'

Her words didn't say anything about the nightmare of being in a deserted spaceship just like theirs . . . about the freezing ghost-haunted blackness, lit only by torchlight, the terrible sense of going into the unknown. And in the NUN chamber they had found something that was still a mystery.

'There were six crystal caskets, exactly like the ones on our ship. Four of them were empty, but two . . .' She paused for a long minute and I could hear her breathing as she relieved the horror. ' . . . Inside the last two, I saw Reb and myself as adults, in deep sleep. Ourselves.'

That Deepwater crew was cloned from the same gene cells. They did not know what had happened to the other four. Or why the adult Yoona and Reb were back in their caskets. The NUN bio-computer on that ship was dying, the COL probably dead.

'Maybe us being there somehow hastened the end. Anyway, the spaceship began to break up and we had to get out – quickly.'

'The caskets?' I whispered.

'They were still on the ship when it destructed.' I could hardly hear her voice on the intercom. The adult Yoona was exactly identical, so it must have been like losing a twin sister.

Yoona stopped talking. I sat there, letting those unreal images steal through my mind as, slowly, our little metal crayfish glided up to the side of the other Deepwater. Bits and pieces of wreckage hung in the blackness and we nudged slowly through them to the black hole of the entrance port – and those little round clusters of . . . space rock?

Yoona slipped her hand into a sensor-glove and moved out one long OMA pincer-claw. She tapped one of the round balls with the claw and it moved to one side but nothing happened.

'Careful!' snapped Reb's voice urgently in the intercom.

'We have to know what it is,' said Yoona.

She reached out the OMA claw again and gently caught the space rock. Her hand squeezed in the sensor-glove and the claw began to squeeze. I remembered how that claw had nipped my ankle. Suddenly the grey ball burst and I jumped. There was a collective gasp from the intercom.

A shower of grey dust fell out. I heard Yoona's sigh of relief and put my hand in the sensor-glove at my side. I selected another globe and squeezed the claw-hand tight. Another crack and shower of grey dust. Just to be sure, we broke several more but they were all the same. Dead chunks of space rock collecting like driftwood round the dead spaceship.

'Sorry, Bren, no junior amebs.' Yoona sounded very relieved though.

'Be careful anyway,' came Reb tensely.

'We will.'

There was no need to go through the port. The whole side of this Deepwater gaped open round huge broken rib-bones of steel. We nudged and clinked our way through the puddle of broken silver-plate and through into the spaceship.

Yoona switched on the bow lights and lit a long white finger ahead. It was like entering the body of a giant whale. We moved silently into what had been the NUN chamber. Now it was split and crumpled like a huge shoe-box somebody had stepped on, and crystal fragments from the NUN door floated like ice in the light. The long centre walkway that led across the top of the spaceship was broken and had drifted down.

I pointed and Yoona nosed the OMA through the broken pieces of the rain-crystal door. Huge chunks of rain-crystal, big enough to crush the OMA, hung without moving in the blackness. There were no forcefields now, but the OMA light glinted a moment on something black below. That mysterious black floor I had walked across. And suddenly I felt a tugging, jerking force coming up through it as though someone was shaking me, trying to get my attention. I jerked in my seat and my head suddenly pounded. I heard Yoona call to me, then everything spun quickly.

Oh no, not now!

I reached out to grab something and jolted again. Chibbi's voice said something about 'Careful, you'll fall off the stool', and I opened my eyes.

We were in the lab. It was another day, I knew, because we had on different clothes. I had some open textbooks and was making notes and I pushed them away, glaring at Chibbi in shock.

'Denie, are you all right?'

'No.' I couldn't be here now! 'I'm with Yoona on Deepwater.'

I squeezed my eyes back shut and grabbed the edges of

109

the bench for support. Inside me, that dizzy feeling was slowing down and I knew that when it stopped I would have to live the prex through. I heard Chibbi call my name again; I felt her hands on mine, but I just made an intense effort to speed up again. Prexing was a state of mind, and I had to get back. I had to push that unstoppable merry-go-round back a moment – but only a moment. Chibbi's hand was still on my arm. I heard Chibbi's voice again and opened my eyes, but into darkness and the sudden flash of light.

'Denie!' It was Yoona's voice, and the flash was torchlight on my visor. She had opened her cover and mine and was standing up, leaning over. She sounded frightened and desperate.

'I'm all right.'

'I thought you'd prexed.'

'I did. I'm OK now.'

Yoona flashed her torch on my face-mask again and nodded. She moved the OMA further forward, away from those rain-crystal pieces and the black floor. I had a tingling strange little feeling that the power under that floor had helped stop my prex. But how? There was no time to think about it, for we were at the opening of the gene tunnel now. The force-wall protecting it seemed to have disappeared. Then the OMA bow light picked out something ahead that glinted.

'Might just be a piece of rain-crystal,' said Yoona. She still sounded breathless. I must have given her a hell of a fright. 'Check it.'

I put out my OMA claw and gently nipped the tiny something, then pulled in the length of the claw. I reached out and pulled it clear and passed it over to Yoona. A gene capsule, but punctured and broken. Trites.

'We've found a gene capsule,' said Yoona. 'Dead.'

Tension and disappointment came back through the intercom like spoken words. Then Gret said, 'Yoona, there are still no life readings, but I'm getting a slight power build-

110

up. Something must be still operating in the spaceship or there's an unknown energy source.' Like from an unknown alien creature?

'Stand by for a quick getaway, people.' That was from Lis.

'Denie, do you want to go on?' Yoona's torch flashed on my helmet like a question mark.

'Yes.' I didn't, of course. It was awful in here, freezing, black and terrifying, like standing in a grave at midnight in winter. But we had to see this through.

Yoona nudged the OMA further into the twisting gene tunnel. And now the nightmares really started. All round us were the hundreds of holes and the crystal-tipped capsules floating in the air. All flattened, punctured and broken, each one a life lost, never to be born. Sometimes they bumped into one another or the OMA and the identifying hologram in the crystal head was activated, flicking on. Asian, African, European, all nations, men, women and children, hundreds and hundreds of them looking at us, then flicking out like pale ghost flames.

'There must be some left, there must be,' whispered Yoona.

But there weren't. All the capsules were broken and all those smiling faces flicked on and off in the darkness like the dead souls they were. There were still flickers of light remaining from the bright river that had once flowed through this tunnel. Sparkling droplets forming into small puddles as though the spaceship was still weeping bright tears for all the lives lost in this blackness. We were at the end of the tunnel now and Yoona cut the OMA engine. She stood, flashing her torch around one last time.

'Nothing,' she said.

I stood up and flashed mine around. It was futile. This was the end of our voyage, the end of all our hopes. We both sat down again and I felt the tears go running down my cheeks. The same word formed in my mouth.

111

'Nothing.'

I could hear Yoona crying too. Nobody spoke on the intercom and round us was the cold, dark closeness of death, lit only by the small puddles and tiny specks of light. Those lights mean something, I was saying inside me, they mean the spaceship is still a tiny bit alive. But everything inside was dead, so they were as much use as candles on a coffin.

'Yoona.'

I didn't know why I spoke. Then I stood up and pointed. Through the tiny tear streaks and puddles of light was a longer, sharper edge that suddenly seemed to show itself among them. I shone my torch over and it flashed on the airlock opening at the end. The long gleam of light was coming from behind that!

'Denie, hold the OMA.'

Yoona's scream nearly made me drop my torch. She was getting out. I couldn't hear anything but imagined her metal boots clanging on the deck. She was kicking aside the punctured capsules and dead faces flicked up at her. Now she was at the airlock and a sudden strong gleam of light came through as she pushed it open. She reached inside and I heard her gasp on the intercom. Then she came back with something in her hand and held it out to show me.

It was a gene capsule, whole and perfect. I pressed the crystal top and a face appeared in the blackness: an Asian child's face, open-mouthed and laughing – and this one glowed like a bright healthy flame in the darkness.

'We've found one,' she said into the intercom and the tears were just as bright in her voice. 'There might be others.'

She put it in the OMA like it was a very precious jewel. Then she waved her hand at me to stay where I was and went back to the airlock hatch. This time she pushed right through and it closed behind her for a minute. And she came back with a handful.

I could only guess how it had happened. I suppose when the ship broke up, the systems went haywire and scattered the gene capsules like confetti. The airlocks must have opened long enough for some to float through and escape being eaten by trites or anything else. And with them was enough of that wonderful water light to keep them alive. But only some of them. The gene banks held hundreds of thousands of those capsules, but Yoona went through the airlock less than a dozen times to come back with hands full of glittering life – only twice with a double handful gleaming in the darkness – a billion times more precious than diamonds.

The last time she was away too long. I waited anxiously and could hear my inner voice telling me to get out, that there was a nightmare something in this huge silent coffin. Then Yoona came back with a single gene capsule and dropped it in my hands. She shook her helmeted head.

'That's all,' she said, then into the intercom, 'Coming out.'

I held it in my hand for a moment. It was about two centimetres long, thick as a nail, with a diamond head. The torchlight showed a programme bar and number stamped along it. 7777777. Seven sevens. Somebody's life in my hands. Yoona had gone through all the exhaust airlocks to find this one last gene. I nearly pressed the crystal to find out who was sleeping, then dropped it in my pouch. I didn't want to know.

We couldn't turn in the gene tunnel. Yoona backed the OMA and I stood with my torch, directing her. The gene pouch was at my feet. They were a few drops of water light, not the rainstorm we had hoped for. Were they enough?

'Patterns,' whispered Yoona. 'The extra two caskets on our ship. You coming out late. Even the way these gene cells survived. There's so much we still don't know.'

'We got the human race back. We know that.'

'Yes, we did, you ass-kicking Earthkid.'

I couldn't see her face, but I knew she was grinning. Now the OMA was back in the wrecked NUN chamber.

Floating pieces of rain-crystal flashed in the OMA bow light as we turned round. Then, from ahead, we sensed rather than felt the movement of something crashing slowly down.

'What was that?' I said.

'The ship must be very unstable,' said Yoona.

Maybe so, I thought, but it was picking one hell of a time. Yoona was still turning the OMA to line up with outside. Now we could see a section of crossbeam floating lazily down and Yoona backed the OMA frantically. Floating, yes, but it would have pinned us like a steel-boned claw. It landed on that black floor behind us and everything seemed to ripple like a shockwave. For a single instant in the blackness, a woman was looking at me, brown-haired, sharp-faced and smiling like we were friends – then she vanished in another black ripple.

'Yoona – did you see that?'

'What?' She twisted round in her seat.

I made to tell her, then actually forgot what I'd seen – because ahead, the bow light of the turning OMA was outlining two crystal caskets, floating, torn loose from the bucking floor. I heard Yoona gasp – she had seen them too. But now the bow light was gleaming off huge, steel girder-bones and she steered for the gap of twinkling black space between them. We both breathed a long sigh of relief as, through the opening, we saw the long bulk of our Deepwater.

'Scannings report everything clear,' came Reb's voice.

'On our way back, Reb,' said Yoona.

There was no time to think about those caskets. Getting the gene pouch into Deepwater and our own gene bank was too important. Then I remembered that vision I had seen. Maybe a full-sized gene-hologram or even an hallucination. But the face looked maddeningly familiar, as though I'd seen her somewhere before. We were nearly up to the girders now and I didn't want to think about it – or those crystal caskets. Surely nobody could be alive in them after so long.

Suddenly the bow light was shining on another cluster

114

of those little space rock things. I opened my mouth to warn Yoona, but it was too late. The pincer-arm on her side touched one, the claw-hand catching and knocking it hard against the others. Tiny cracks appeared all over them.

'Life-readings,' screamed Gret from Deepwater.

But we already knew what those things were as they split open. No showers of dust this time because these ones were not dead. They were very much alive. They were eggs and they were hatching.

Yoona put on speed to get clear of the opening. But the first shell cracked and a round, light grey object hurtled out and bounced against the OMA. It unfolded itself and flapped wings, the light grey going dark, the eyes coming out on stalks. The OMA claw caught on some wreckage and Yoona stopped for a moment, frantically trying to clear it.

It took only a moment but it was long enough for the other eggs to crack open – and for all the other trites to come tumbling out, spreading their wings and already full of horrible life.

15 Monster from the death ship

'Get clear!' we heard Reb shout. Lis could not fire on the trites without hitting us. Yoona opened the OMA to full power, but those things were already moving fast. More than twenty of them, hatched fully-grown in deep space and spreading out round us.

It was no use closing the hatch, for they would smash the thin glass. I unslung my laser rifle and pressed the button at the end. It nearly jolted out of my hand as a thin yellow streak of laser jetted out at the trites. One of them spun sharply, then we were clear of the wreck. They came streaming after us, circling and ready to dive.

Yoona put the OMA in such a tight curve that I nearly fell out. I blazed my laser round and the circle broke up. Yoona took the OMA in a circling dive and I fired the laser again. One of them crashed down between us and I swiped it off. Then three more, two at me and one at Yoona. The OMA bucked as she took her hands off the controls, nearly throwing us both this time. More of the trites were diving.

Then a blast of laser fire splattered round them and they went in all directions. Another OMA sailed past, the cover up and Gret flying it. Bren stood beside her, firing his laser. Behind them, out of Deepwater's port, came Reb and Lis. Deepwater was open and helpless behind them, but that didn't matter. If we couldn't save the genes, we might as well die in space with them.

I pulled the trite off as its drill-sting arched. The steel hook legs tore at my space suit. Gret spun her OMA round in a tight curve beside us as I leaned over and grabbed Yoona's trite. Yoona slipped her hand in the sensor-glove and locked our OMA with Gret's, claw-in-claw. Reb zoomed up on the other side and locked pincers with me. Yoona, Reb and Gret stood facing one way, me, Lis and Bren the other. The trites came in to attack and our lasers flashed a criss-cross of yellow streaks in the blackness.

In a minute it was all over. The trites came for us like wasps for jam and it was them or us. We blasted away at point-blank range and it made me sick, but this was one battle we had to win. And when it was finished, we just sat there, hearing each other's breathless gasps on the intercom. I opened my hand and let my rifle go, not caring if I never saw it again.

'Reb.' Yoona closed the OMA up as far as she could and handed the precious gene pouch over.

'Get them back and check for trites inside. And wait.'

'What are you doing?' Gret was still standing and turned her helmeted head towards us.

Yoona looked at me before she answered and I nodded. I knew what she wanted to do.

'We're going back into the spaceship. Those two closed caskets are still there.'

They didn't say anything. Something really close was bonding us now and we didn't need a lot of words. It was like when the others got into their space suits and made the OMAs ready, just in case we would need them. They didn't know about the trites, they just wanted to be ready. And they understood now.

We unlinked OMA claws and the other two closed covers, heading back to Deepwater. We turned back to the wreck, through the girders and the cluster of broken trite eggs. The steel bones of this Deepwater closed round us again and Yoona took the OMA through the darkness of the ruined NUN chamber. Ahead in the OMA bow light were the two rain-crystal caskets, floating side by side.

118

Yoona opened the cover and passed me her laser rifle. She got out on to the floor of the NUN chamber and linked each casket with a towing chain from the back of the OMA.

'Can you see anyone in them?' I whispered.

'No,' she said. 'Too dark.'

'Deepwater secure,' came Reb's voice on the intercom. Something else floated down beside us and the dark spaceship seemed to move slightly. Pieces of shattered casket jiggled up and down like ice-cubes in black water. And that voice was back inside me, my voice, saying danger, danger, danger.

'Coming out,' said Yoona.

She got back into the OMA and closed the cover. Now we were moving back to the opening. Then something else crashed lazily down and the broken arches shook.

'Reb, can you see what's happening?'

'No. The spaceship's moving a bit, more at the bow end. Get out!'

Yoona set the OMA straight at the gap and we crashed through among the broken pieces of silver-plate. Then suddenly the whole side of the ship seemed to turn and out of the shattered cabin oozed a grey-white mass.

'Ameb!' shouted Reb.

'Reb, get moving, that's an order,' Yoona screamed at once. 'Move, move, that's an order!'

'I'll try and come back for you.'

'No you won't!' Yoona was almost crying with tension as she took the OMA down under the rolling spaceship to hide us. 'Get away – get away – order, order!'

Deepwater was already turning and speeding off. There was no way they could wait for us, or reach us. Amebs were just too dangerous. Reb tried to say something else, but it was lost as the range out-distanced our small OMA receiver.

The ameb was reforming itself in outer space. The sounds of battle or a stray laser blast must have woken it up. It was bigger than any she had ever seen, whispered Yoona, and backed the OMA well underneath. But the thing wasn't interested in us. It set off after Deepwater, moving with incredible speed. In moments, both were lost from sight.

'Maybe Reb will find a way back.' Even as I said that, I knew it was stupid.

'COL's programming won't let Deepwater turn round. Bren tried once.' Her gloved hand came out and took mine. 'Impossible.'

The Deepwater arks were not meant to do anything but go on to their destination. It was very cold in the OMA and we had about an hour of life left. I looked back at the two rain-crystal caskets we were still towing. There might be back-up systems in their caskets, but they wouldn't last long either. If they were still alive.

'Thanks for everything, Denie.'

'My privilege, Yoona.'

We were silent for a few minutes to save air. Anyway, there was nothing to say. Somewhere and already thousands of kilometres distant, Reb and the others were running for their lives. They couldn't put Deepwater into time-blink until they were past the next colour-reef and we had seen how fast that ameb could move.

'Can they outrun it?' It didn't matter about saving air.

Yoona was looking ahead. She took the OMA in another turn under the belly of the dead spaceship and said, in a very matter-of-fact but tense tone, 'They must have. It's coming back.'

The ameb was a pale, splotchy, grey-white colour like it had spent too long inside the dark space suit. It was humped at the front and tailed the rest of its body in long tentacles. Yoona took the OMA further down and the spaceship shook round us as the thing settled again. We thought we had managed to hide in time, but a pale, grey-white tentacle arm came snaking down under the ship and Yoona turned the OMA tightly again.

Another came down the other side. She ducked ahead, but both tentacle arms moved with us and Yoona took the OMA up into the broken spaceship, like a little crab trying to escape an octopus in a sunken liner. But this octopus was big and clever, the sunken liner was its home and it knew just where to look. We were in the centre, back in the NUN chamber, and the grey-white mass came oozing after us, like elastic clay.

We shot out the other side and another groping tentacle just missed us. The whole mass of the thing was sitting on top of the spaceship and seemed to gather itself like a horrible snowball, rolling down the side. We had nowhere to hide and Yoona took the OMA out into deep space again, the wake-up caskets trailing behind.

The ameb slipped off the spaceship in a thick mass. Huge tentacle arms spread on either side and it moved forward, towering over us. Yoona gasped and pushed the control stick forward but we couldn't go any faster. We couldn't escape and somehow the thing sensed it. The tentacle arms began to wrap round, then its whole grey-white mass shuddered as something just as big rammed the ameb from behind and smashed it aside.

Deepwater!

'Get clear!' came Reb's yell and straight after that, the boom-boom of the laser cannon.

I had read about fights between giant squids and whales in the black depths of the ocean. It was like that now, in the black depths of outer space, but these opponents were fifty times stronger and more massive than the biggest whale or squid. The ameb forgot us and turned, reforming itself. Deepwater spun round and the battle begun.

Reb was flying Deepwater in a wide circle round us. The ameb followed and each time it drew close, Reb blasted it with engine force and threw it back. And in the bubble-turret, Lis – it had to be Lis – fired blast after blast of yellow laser fire straight into it. But this ameb was very big and very tough. It soaked up the punishment like a sponge and kept coming.

Suddenly the ameb shot across the circle and threw part of itself at Deepwater like a loop in a rope. Reb ducked the spaceship underneath, and we could hear the non-stop yell of his orders to COL as he missed the trap. He turned Deepwater round again and suddenly rammed the ameb, pushing it back. Then he spun and reversed, slamming another engine-blast into the ameb at close range like a well-aimed fist at a punching-bag. He took Deepwater in another circle but the ameb did not follow. It was sagging like a cushion with the stuffing knocked out. Lis pounded it with laser cannon and it seemed to collapse.

'Stand by.'

Reb was turning Deepwater round and heading for us. Yoona waited, then headed straight for the opening port. Deepwater slowed a moment and she shot inside, the caskets bouncing behind us. The port cartwheeled shut and Lis screamed through the intercom.

'It's coming back!'

The overhead boom-boom of the laser fired again as Yoona and I threw ourselves out of the OMA and through the opening airlocks, stripping off our space suits as we did. The last airlock was still sliding shut as Yoona, her blonde hair flying, threw herself across the lower deck and up the stairs. We were halfway over the upper deck when Deepwater shuddered and stopped. We were thrown to the floor, but Yoona got up and flung herself into the control chair.

'COL, voice-ac!' she yelled and the console glowed red. 'COL, full speed ahead, vision screen rear section.' But the spaceship did not move and the vision screen flickered into a terrifying image. The ameb, not as beaten as it had looked, had wrapped part of its body round Deepwater and hooked a long, thick tentacle to the other spaceship, holding them both together.

'COL, full power!' yelled Yoona, her body forward, both hands gripping the console.

It was no use. The ameb was super-strong and had a tight hold. Deepwater was straining against a massive bodyweight and the dead anchor of its own twin. Already Deepwater's hull was straining and creaking under the enormous squeezing pressure of the monster. And the ship was hotter becuase the ameb was locked over our tail section. The exhaust fumes had nowhere to go and were heating up the pipes, then the shafts – and then us. Overhead came the boom-boom and Lis yelled into the intercom.

'Yoona, I'm not even denting it!'

At full power, we could not even move forward. Even blasts of energy-force could not shake it now. Then little by little, the ameb began pulling us back.

16   Deepwater sun storm

We could hear the ship straining as though trying to breathe.
The control deck was hotter already. I was kneeling between
the control chairs and Reb grabbed my arm as the deck
slanted and Deepwater moved back again.

'We can't move while it's holding the other ship,' he
yelled. Yoona nodded, white-faced.

I don't know what made me think of it – the idea just
flashed into my mind like an on-screen computer print-out.
'Ask COL.' The words flicked off my tongue. 'Can it contact
that other ship?'

'What do you mean?' Yoona was still gripping the console
tight.

'That water light round the gene capsules . . . maybe their
COL is somehow still alive.'

Deepwater strained again, still shuddering to break free
from the ameb's choking embrace. Now it was very hot.

'How does that help us?' shouted Gret.

I was trying to think. Something inside was telling me,
like busy thought-fingers pushing the puzzle pieces together.
Lis screamed through the intercom again.

'That thing is coming up the side!'

The vision screen showed the ameb slowly crawling up
the length of Deepwater, dragging the other spaceship behind
it.

'Lis, get out of the bubble, we'll seal.' The ameb would
crack it like an eggshell.

'No!' Her voice shook but she sounded brave. 'I'm

staying, I can slow it down.' The laser went boom-boom again and the top hatch slid shut with a thud. She had sealed herself up.

'Lis . . .' began Yoona and I interrupted.

'Yoona!' It was coming out in thought-clicking flashes now. 'We can contact the COL on that other ship – tell it to self-destruct!'

'Crazy,' muttered Bren.

'No!' I *knew* all this, it was thought-clicking in my head. 'Life preservation is the primary programme – now ours has the gene bank, so the other COL will protect it.'

Deepwater croaked again and the laser cannon kept pounding. But it was only slowing the ameb down, not stopping it. Before long the heat would roast us or the thing would smash through the iron-glass.

'COL.' Yoona spoke quickly. The floor was already warm and turning a funny colour. 'Can you contact the COL on that other ship?'

'Yes,' said that super-cool voice. And I wanted to yell, so why not tell us before?

'COL, tell it we have removed all that is left of the gene bank. Tell it the gene bank is in danger, and it is stopping us escaping.' She shut her eyes a moment. 'Tell it to self-destruct – ask it to save us!'

The hull creaked again with a nasty little snapping sound like the time I broke my collar bone. The floor was hot and the walls were changing colour as they heated. Lis came on the intercom, that brave tremble in her voice.

'I can only hold it a few moments longer, Yoona.'

'COL, did you pass that message?' yelled Yoona.

'Yes.'

Oh, that stupid computer. What did 'yes' mean? Probably that the other COL just said 'yes', too, then might think about it for a few years before *doing* anything! 'Good one, Denie,' said my voice clearly in my head – and what the hell was I saying *that* for? This was anything but a good one . . .

126

A sunburst of intense golden light flooded across our vision screen and eye-windows, even inside, bursting, blinding and dazzling us in solid flaming yellow. Sound cannot carry in the vacuum of outer space but, through the ship, a rolling sonic thunder smashed against our eardrums. And there was no shockwaves in outer space, but something hit us so hard that Deepwater was flung crazily sideways like a skittle hit by a bowling ball and sliding over a black polished floor.

The other Deepwater had exploded. All we could see was a huge ball of light, shimmering in golden layers and of the ameb, there was no sign. It had taken the full impact and been flicked away like a wet rag. Deepwater stopped sliding and Yoona screamed into the intercom.

'Lis, are you all right?'

We waited an endless, unbearable second before a tiny choked voice answered, 'Yes.'

Deepwater shuddered again and settled. Outside in space, the golden light ball was fading into nothing – nothing. The other Deepwater had vanished.

I could hear a stifled sound on the intercom and knew Lis was crying. Gret bent her head over her console and let her green hair fall about her face. Bren tugged hard on one dreadlock and slammed his hand hard on the arm-rest. Reb just sat there looking at the screen, and Yoona took her hands from the console and pressed them over her face.

I felt something too, as though a little patch had gone empty in my mind. As though I'd just lost someone very close to me.

Yoona was the first to recover. She had to swallow several times before she spoke. 'COL, on course, cruising speed.'

The spaceship settled again and began moving. I couldn't shake off that awful feeling of loss or understand why I felt it so deeply. Deepwater didn't seem any the worse, but Yoona took COL through a complex set of questions about hull structure, vents, engines, before she relaxed slightly. Then she sat up again, remembering something.

'We'd better get the genes into our support system and lock in COL.' Then remembering something else, in a grimmer tone, 'Reb, I told you not to come back.'

'We all agreed to come back,' snapped Gret, just beating Bren to the same words.

'Yes,' said Lis through the intercom, adding some low words that sounded like, 'so shut up, Yoona.'

Yoona's beautiful golden-brown complexion went red. 'All right.' She swallowed again, then remembered something else. 'And *how* did you turn Deepwater round?'

'I didn't really.' Reb was still white-faced and his voice shook. 'I just told COL to take Deepwater in a circle, a big circle. Then time-blinked to try and lose the ameb. It was simple.'

Oh, yes, simple. So simple that Yoona leaned over and gave him a big hug. He went red and then I gave him a hug and he went redder. But we only forgot for a moment what had happened.

'COL, switch off the screen.'

It went blank. The other Deepwater, the other COL, had saved us. Yes, the people who built and programmed these spaceships really did think of everything.

Everything?

The two caskets in the main port. Before we did anything else, even before telling Lis what a hero she was, we had to check them.

Yoona transferred voice-ac back to Reb. 'Keep scanning. We don't know if the ameb really is gone. And do another hull check. Denie and I will get the gene bank running.'

We went below deck and through the airlocks. I was having a small sense of unease. We had talked about patterns and everything being planned – but did that include salvaging those caskets? And I was getting more uneasy about what we would find in them. The last airlock opened into the port where the battle-scarred OMA rested beside the two crystal caskets. But they were open and empty. And the gene pouch was gone.

Then Reb's voice came urgently on the intercom. 'Yoona, the gene bank has been operated.'

We looked at each other, then ran back through the airlocks to the lower deck. We were going back up the steps and heard something click behind. It was the door from the NUN corridor opening. And a woman's voice, amused and cold: 'Looking for us?'

We turned very slowly. Two adults were standing there and the woman spoke again. 'All that crashing around activated our wake-ups. So we put the genes away.'

'Let's get on deck,' said the man.

Yoona and I stood glued for a moment, then went up the stairs. The adults followed, stepping out on deck like they owned it. The others, especially Reb, got as big a shock as we did. Because he and Yoona were looking at themselves.

Both adults were nearly two metres tall, long somehow, and very slim with sharp features. They were adult long-haired copies of Reb and Yoona and identical – but different. Two words came to my mind. Attenuated and translucent. That was how they looked.

Attenuated; drawn-out, stretched, and they were both so slim. That was how they looked. Fine-boned, my mum said when she used the word to describe a woman blues singer. And translucent, as though the life in their bodies was shining through their tight skin. Their eyes were bright and neither of them seemed to mind the dead silence at all.

'You gave us quite a battering on the way over,' said the adult Yoona.

'We were attacked by an ameb,' said our Yoona. 'A very big one from inside the spaceship.'

'And you got rid of it in a very clever way,' said the adult Reb.

'Yes. Whose idea was that?' said the adult Yoona. Just in the way they spoke, they were already taking over.

'Denie's,' said Yoona.

Reb had whispered a holding pattern to COL. Lis had come to the top of the stairs and there was a strange stiff tension through the deck. There was something unclose and cold about these two and they looked . . . wrong. Clone-brother and clone-sister they might be to our Reb and Yoona, but they were also – different.

'Denie?' said the woman. She looked at me. Yoona's eyes were full of golden warmth but hers were like dead yellow stones.

'Denie . . .' echoed the adult Reb. There was a strangeness in the way they both said it. 'Yes, we know about Denie.'

There was still that uncanny silence in Deepwater. Gret was scanning and Lis was back in the bubble because we could not relax our watch. But they were still listening to the adults and the way they spoke. Their voices were full of secrets.

The woman walked up with all the grace of a ballerina. She looked amused again, the way a cat looks when it plays with a mouse. 'I'll tell you about it when you've finished prexing.'

'She means you're about to prex again,' said adult Reb. Their voices were high like overstrung guitars. He folded his arms and looked at me the same way.

It was as though they set something off. My head spun and I staggered. Yoona caught me and Reb came running over. I'd been expecting this, as I'd somehow stopped one prex and it was bound to catch up with me. But the sudden sick buzzing burst loudly round me and now the whole deck whirled round me. I couldn't speak and the strong, vivid images of those clone-adults seemed to spin with me, fine, pale faces and grinning mouths, like a living nightmare.

Then it all went black.

17   Reeboks springs a trap

When I opened my eyes, I was looking at an image in a square frame. It was in colour, sharp and flickery, and everything was misty round it. Then the mistiness went away and a woman with a weather chart came into the picture.

I was watching television.

'Enjoy dinner?' asked Mum as she took away an empty plate from my knees. She smiled like everything was normal.

'Sure, Mum, thanks,' I replied mechanically. I was in my nightie and Dad was asleep in the other chair. He always falls asleep during the TV news and says he would go mad otherwise.

Mum came back with coffee and sat down beside me. She put an arm round my shoulders and gave me a quick kiss.

'You had a visitor this afternoon.' She used the remote to terminate the weather report. 'You were asleep.'

'Chibbi?' I said.

'No, the boy – he calls himself Meatground?'

'Meatgrinder?'

So what did he want? Come to think of it, I felt weak and somehow drained. Had I been sick again? I sipped my coffee.

'He just wanted to know how you were.'

'Ah, what did you tell him, Mum?'

'Just that you'd passed a feverish night and day when Chibbi bought you back from the lab. He brought a chocolate bar but I was a bit hungry and I ate it.' She grinned without any feeling of guilt. 'Robbie's been too, and Ms Booth.'

'Did you score their chocolate bars too?'

Mum's grin seemed to fix itself for a moment, then she leaned over and gave me a tight, tight hug. One little tear stayed on my cheek when she sat back and blew her nose. 'And Chibbi Orduna called. You two seem to have quite a friendship.'

'She's a good person.' I gave Mum a hug back and then had to blow my nose.

I asked some careful questions, trying not to let slip that my mind was blank. Chibbi said I had become feverish on the way home from the lab – when I nearly prexed in the other Deepwater – and she brought me home. I was put through another medical juicer, but Dad and the other doctors couldn't find anything wrong.

'Denie, we've left you on your own a lot. Too much. So I'm cutting back my work and so is your father. We're going to be more of a family.'

'I'm feeling a lot better, Mum.' Did they think it was all a plea for attention? 'You don't have to do this.'

'Yes, we do.'

Dad woke up and grinned at me and suddenly it was great having two parents who cared so much. Space-side Denie had fought off giant amebs and was having bad trouble with two adult clones, but Earth-side Denie had good years ahead. And Meatgrinder had brought a chocolate bar round! There *was* hope for the human race! All we did was talk before I went to bed and it was just about the best night I could remember.

I had a week off school and went to the institute lab the next morning. The first thing I saw was Chibbi's big silver-ornamented boots on the table. She was putting moccasins on her feet. 'Hi, Denie,' she said, but so casually that I hesitated. Why was she pretending nothing had happened?

'Chibbi, you're not a solid-hologram, are you?'

'Denie!' Chibbi gasped and dropped her moccasin.

Of course I was switched back to the Earth-Denie mode

when she visited me at home. So she was just playing it cool. She sat me down and made me tell her what had happened. She was still asking tricky questions, but I still had that instinct she believed me – despite herself.

'And what now?' she asked quietly, and that brought it all back to me.

'I want to be on Deepwater!' Even with those clone-adults running things, it seemed more real than anything on Earth. I had told her about them and she looked very thoughtful.

'Those adults . . . attenuated?' But she stopped talking, her mouth open and her eyes fixed on mine.

'Chibbi?' I said – and jumped as a long pale hand came down on my shoulder and a high uptight voice spoke behind me.

'She can't hear you. Technically I've stopped your prex, but you're still living it.' Adult Yoona stepped in front, the headband on her blonde and red hair, quick yellow eyes darting round. 'What a primitive place this is.' She was looking at Chibbi as though she were a zoo animal and put out her hand to touch her.

'Leave her!' I snapped.

'Calm down.' She took her hand away, though. 'I never thought I'd prex into the lab of the famous Chibbi.'

'What do you want?'

'This is your last prex, Denie.' Her yellow eyes glowed with cold hypnotic fire. You can stay safe here, your body in the crystal casket on Deepwater. In a safe Earth-dream.'

'Why are you saying this?'

'We don't need you.' Her smile had a lot of sharp white teeth. 'You weren't programmed.'

'Yoona,' I muttered, and that little buzz went on in my head, then stopped. 'Yoona and Reb want me.'

'I am Yoona. I don't.' She took a long step back. 'Goodbye.'

Her hand went to the headband, then her body rippled into an outline of flickering dots that somehow zipped up

133

and vanished. I sat there and let the buzzing in my head stop. Chibbi spoke.

'Denie?'

'She was here, the adult Yoona.' Then I blacked out and was on the couch when I came to. Chibbi was splashing water on my face.

'Sit still,' she said. 'Denie, enough is enough. I'm talking to your parents.'

'No!' I never thought I could shout so loud. 'Chibbi, this is just you and me! That adult Yoona knew you, and something very big is coming from all this. This is you and me and nobody else – nobody!'

I must have been yelling at the top of my voice because somebody poked their head round the door and asked if everything was OK. Chibbi nodded and the somebody went. Then she sat thinking. I don't think it was my anger – I think it was her mother's blood telling her something. And Chibbi had always listened to her mother.

'I didn't know you for a moment,' she said.

'I'm still Denie. I'm just trying to make this thing work.'

Chibbi nodded and just for a second there was a cut-out line round her, as though she was a photo stuck on paper. Reb had told me what that meant. My prex would climax as his did – but he had Yoona to boost him out if things went wrong. Now I had nobody.

'I'll come home with you, Denie.'

'I've got things to do.' I didn't even know what those things were. I just had an overwhelming sense that time was running out.

'I'll see you again, though?'

I nodded, but I got that vibe again. I'd be Earth-Denie the next time she saw me, with no memory. This was the last time she'd see Denie from across time and space. I think she sensed that.

'I still don't know what to believe,' she said. Then she gently put out a hand and plucked a hair from my head. She smiled, standing with the light behind her. 'That's all it takes for a gene. I'll keep yours safe. Be strong, *compañera*.'

'Goodbye, Chibbi.'

We hugged each other tight and I felt a little tear on my cheek, just like Mum. I left one on her cheek too. Then I turned and left without looking back because I wanted my last picture to be Chibbi standing with the sunlight round her.

Cycling away from the gym, I had a terrible feeling that a time fuse was burning and there was something I hadn't done. I stopped my bike, shut my eyes tight and my head spun again. Then a name inputted like data in my mind – and why *that* name?

Connal. As in Meatgrinder.

On Deepwater they might already be putting my Cei-body in the crystal casket. But I had to do this one thing, I had to find Connal – even if I had no idea what to say to him. I cycled into the shopping centre near our school. There were some kids there on bikes, with milkshakes. Robbie was among them and he came over.

'Denie . . . ah, we've got a party tonight, after the match. Would you like to come?'

This was getting unreal and crazy. Robbie, I nearly said, your space-side just fought a battle with an alien monster. You and me are part of the struggle to keep our human race alive. And Earth-side, I was thinking how to lay it on Mum and Dad for some new gear.

'Sure, I'd like that. Have you seen Connal?'

'He's in the park,' came a voice behind. Reeboks. He gave me a funny look and cycled off.

'Meatgrinder?' Robbie sounded puzzled. 'What do you want him for?'

'Robbie, his name's Connal. Give him a chance.'

'Yeah, well, keep clear. You know why Reeboks told you? Because somebody paint-bombed Meatgrinder's Mum's dairy and he thinks . . .'

'It was me?' Robbie nodded, but I just swung my bike round. 'Doesn't matter, I have to see him.'

'Want me to come?' His eyes flickered a moment in that little memory-click. I just shook my head, smiled and headed for the park.

It was the same place I had mud-pied Reeboks and Connal back in the days when he was still Meatgrinder. I cycled round looking for him, with that urgent feeling inside getting worse. There was a shed the groundsman used at the far side and the door was open. I went over.

'Connal?'

I went inside. Then, from behind, somebody pushed me hard. I landed on a pile of wet sacks and the door slammed. A paper-bag came sailing in the window and split open on the floor. Some spray-cans rolled out and Reeboks' grinning face appeared at the window.

'Hah!' he yelled. 'Meatgrinder's going to find you like that!'

That paint-bombing – the little rat was going to frame me!

Reeboks was jumping up and down in delight. 'He's going to find you. I called the big dumb jerk to come over . . .'

A big pair of hands grabbed his shoulders and a big voice growled aloud, 'So who're you calling a big dumb jerk?' Then the shed door kicked open. Connal was there, holding a struggling, squealing Reeboks.

'She did it, Meatie – caught her, paint-bombs . . .'

My head was doing a giddy blender-spin but somehow inspiration flashed. 'Did I? Connal, he hasn't even got the smarts to take the paint stains off his jeans.'

Reeboks jerked away and looked down, terrified – for just a moment too long, and Connal clicked. I knew he wasn't really dumb! Then Reeboks and Connal weren't doing anything, they had stopped in a freeze-frame and Reb was there, out of nowhere, with the headband on his blue-black hair.

'You've been prexing too long – come on.'

'The adult Yoona . . .'

'Never mind her – come on or you'll stay here.'

'One moment, Reb.' Reeboks and Connal were frozen in the doorway and the room was spinning again.

'A moment too long – come on!' He grabbed my hand.

'No!' I staggered – it was like swimming against a strong undertow. Then I tore my hand from Reb's and the spinning slowed down. Reeboks and Connal speeded up into movement again and I yelled as loud as I could.

'The lab, the place the school went to, talk to Chibbi – talk to Chibbi!' That was it, that was what I *knew* I had to say and I stopped as though my mouth was glued. Reeboks squealed again.

'Don't listen to that dumb girl, Meatgrinder!'

It was wonderful to watch because Meatgrinder turned and gave Reeboks a hard shove that sent him back over the creek bank into the mud. He yelled louder than me.

'My name is Connal!'

My own voice seemed weak and small. 'Yes, and you're a hero, Connal.'

My prex had stopped. I was in my Earth-dream forever, but for this one long heart-beat of time, it didn't matter. Change ourselves and change the world. I opened my mouth to say that and . . .

Something banged into my arm and my head exploded like Colour-space gone mad. Whizz – I was in the blender, spinning so hard my eyeballs bounced, then I crashed on something hard and heard a familiar voice.

'Denie!'

I opened my eyes, back on the narrow below-deck bunk. Reb and Yoona were there. She had on the headband and something like a spark plug in her hand.

'I boosted you back,' she said, sounding almost scared.

'Denie . . . ?' Reb sounded even more scared. I must have looked blank because he used my other name, more sharply. 'Cei . . . ?'

137

They thought I was the wrong one! 'No, you're stuck with Denie.' Their smiles of relief were really nice to see.

Reb gave me a squeeze-bottle. 'We only just boosted you in time.'

'The adults, they tried to . . .'

'We know,' Yoona nodded. 'We pretended to obey, then Lis took adult Yoona into the bubble over something.'

'And Gret fluttered her eyelashes at the adult Reb,' grinned Reb. That must have been something to see.

'So you brought her back.' Adult Yoona had come down the stairs, silent as a cat. She was wearing a small pistol like a mini-laser and kept her hand on it. 'That was very stupid.'

'Denie is part of Deepwater,' said Yoona defiantly.

Adult Yoona showed her white teeth. 'No. She's too dangerous.'

She pulled out the laser pistol.

18   The power rings of COL

I still felt terrible after that prex, as though I was made of
soggy newspaper. Reb pulled me up and he and Yoona
stepped in front of the gun, shielding me with their bodies.

She looked at them both, a moment longer at Yoona then
grinned, still cat-like but with a touch of respect. She waved
the gun at the upper hatch and motioned us to go first. Yoona
took my arm and Reb dropped behind to cover me on the
steps. They really were good crewmates.

There was always some tension on the control deck, but
now you could twang the air like a guitar. Gret and Bren sat
stiffly together and Lis stood beside them. Deepwater was
in a holding pattern and adult Reb was at the controls. There
was a hostile flash in his eyes as he looked at me – and
something else. Fear?

'Explanation time,' said adult Yoona.

'Including her?' He didn't look at me.

'What about me?' I said. I hate being talked over like I
don't exist.

The adult Yoona didn't look at me either. 'The NUN
bio-computer went bad on this ship, didn't it?' She walked
over in a tense, strutting way to stand beside the adult Reb.
'Ours did, too.'

'We destroyed it,' said Yoona.

'In time it will regenerate,' said adult Reb. 'Bio-
computers never quite die.' She pointed at me, still
without looking. 'And it will focus on her because she is
unprogrammed and NUN wants control – domination.'

'Just like humans,' said adult Yoona in her smiling-cat voice. 'We put Denie back in her casket and NUN will have nothing to focus on.' This time they both looked at me.

'This is our Deepwater. We decide that,' said Yoona. All of us were gathered round her now and we looked at the adults across the control deck.

'Listen carefully,' said adult Reb in that cold, dreamy way of theirs. 'We'll only say this once.' His hand stroked his gun holster. Outside, space was totally black and Deepwater moved in an endless circle, the twinkling lights of Colour-space very far distant.

'By the last decade of the twenty-first century – one hundred years on from Denie Miles's own time – Earth was just enclosed cities. Pollution and the greenhouse effect had killed all life outside them. The raw materials from Mars and the asteroid bases were a blood transfusion, but then a mysterious plague wiped out the last Earth-people. Earth died, like an apple rotting on the ground.

'The Martian colonies tried to be self-contained, but none of the four quadrants really like each other and unified government was very difficult.

'North Martians thought the South was trying to dominate them. Sandies and rockheads were never very bright.' Adult Reb's tone was cold and full of contempt. He just smiled at the glares from Lis, Gret and Bren.

And then it didn't matter, he said, because the shadow of death came to Mars. Another plague began on Mars. There was no cure and nobody ever recovered. It was similar to the Earth-plague and was supposed to have started in hybrid flower pollen caused by terraforming. People just went to sleep and never woke up, and soon it was obvious the solar colonies were doomed. Then the quadrants unified, but it was too late. Only one slender and impossible chance remained to save the human race.

Project Deepwater. Two gene arks, one for humans, the second for animals. Propelled by a new energy source that

140

could take them to the ultimate 'time-blinking' super-speed. To follow the circle of the universe through Colour-space to a time-warp black hole that would take them back to Earth a million years in the future. But the dangers of Colour-space were known by then and crews were needed for that last stage of the voyage.

'Our first Deepwater crew cloned from take-off,' said adult Yoona. Her yellow eyes flicked to all of us in turn. 'Deep sleep, then recloning, then deep sleep. Each clone generation passed on its skills to the next so they became even brighter.' And lost a lot of soul, I thought, as the two adults grinned at each other and she went on, 'Reb and I are *very* clever.'

'So clever that you ended up nowhere,' said Gret.

She'd been smarting over that 'sandie' gibe and never used her sharp tongue to better effect. Lis and Bren laughed and a faint touch of colour appeared in adult Yoona's cheeks.

'What happened to the rest of your crew?' asked Yoona.

'One by one they got the pollen virus.' Adult Reb spoke this time and hesitated, as though keeping things back. 'You children were cloned just before Colour-space. But even with deep sleep and time-blinking, we were there much longer. Suddenly there were just two of us.' He stopped for a moment. They both seemed to get tired easily. 'So we decided to go back into deep sleep until we reached Colour-space. We created solid-holograms with an intelligence programme as our crew.'

Solid-holograms! Their NUN would have created those.

'We linked NUN to the COL circuits so the hologram-crew could stay together outside the NUN chamber.' Adult Yoona was speaking again. 'Perhaps the ports opened somehow by accident. That would have dematerialised their body structure.'

'Did COL destroy them?' The words just clicked off my tongue.

'What do you know about COL?' Adult Yoona's voice went to a high screech. 'She goes back to her casket – now!'

'We decide that!' said Yoona.

'No, we do!' Adult Yoona was spitting her words out. 'Your COL will respond to my voice – *we* are in command, children.'

'Children?' yelled Reb incredulously.

'Yes, children!' snapped his adult clone in exactly the same way.

'You don't give orders!' shouted Bren.

'We give *you* nothing but orders!' Adult Reb looked vicious and mean. 'And you. And you.' He pointed in turn to Lis and Gret. There was a sudden silence. Maybe it was distant gene memory, but we all sensed he was going to say something horrible. He was.

'NUN was programmed not to tell the truth about your skin colours. Red, blue and green?' He gave that horrible white-toothed grin again. 'Sun filters, ozone layers? North Martians and Jupies were cloned like that. To keep them apart, keep them on their colonies – workers and miners!'

'Not good enough for you puddle-bunnies!' screamed Gret, her green eyes on fire. His words had unlocked a data bank of bitter gene memories.

'Yes.' Adult Reb gave a cold smile. 'Freakies – sandies and rockheads.'

That did it. Bren stepped forward and swung his fist, his face even redder with anger. Adult Reb just stepped back with super-quick reflexes and Bren followed with a hard kick. Adult Reb sidestepped super-fast again, grabbed Bren's foot and twisted it hard. I almost heard the ankle bone crack as Bren flew through the air and hit the metal walls with a crash. Blood stained his dreadlocks another red. He tried to get up and his badly-twisted ankle gave way.

Gret had flung herself on adult Yoona just as quickly.

She got what seemed a light push but staggered back across the deck, cannoning into Lis. Both fell. Adult Reb's gun was already in his hand, pointing at Yoona and Reb.

'Denie goes back into her casket – now!' he said.

'Yes, Denie, you must.'

I couldn't believe it was our Yoona who said that. Neither could Gret, kneeling beside Bren. 'It didn't take you long, puddle-bunnie,' she screamed.

'She's remembered who she is,' cat-smiled adult Yoona.

'Yes.' Our Yoona gave a superior smile. 'I'm a South Martian.' Reb and I were still gaping at her as she turned and dropped her voice to an urgent whisper. 'Denie – find COL!'

Her foot was already stamping on the deck button and I dived through the hatch like a rocket. Yoona's foot stamped again and the hatch cut off an angry high yell from adult Reb. I hit the bottom nearly as hard as Bren hit the wall and threw myself over at the NUN door, slapping my hand in the palm-print lock. Behind me, the hatch opened again as I ran through the NUN door.

The corridor leading to the NUN chamber was about half a kilometre long. I was always a good runner, but this time I had to outrun even a laser blast. I ran as hard and fast as I could, not knowing how long the others could block those adults. They must have put up a good fight because I was nearly at the other end before I heard the light running footsteps behind me. I slammed my hand on to another palm lock and, as the door opened, risked a look back.

Behind, running like a panther, came adult Yoona, her blonde hair flying, mouth in a snarl and eyes burning yellow diamonds. One arm was out. I didn't see the gun and didn't wait. I slammed the door and pounded across the empty expanse of the NUN chamber.

But running to where? Find COL, Yoona had said. But COL had never let us find it, never answered questions, never helped us do anything except run the spaceship. That and keep the gene cargo secure . . .

'COL!' I screamed and my voice came back in mocking echoes. 'COL, help me – I think our mission is being threatened.' Nothing. Maybe the mission wasn't being threatened – and there was nowhere to hide in the NUN chamber!

'COL!' I screamed again, 'Please!'

The same mocking echoes were split by a high blood-hunting shriek.

'Denie!'

Adult Yoona was in the NUN chamber. Now her hair hung tangled round her face and those terrible yellow eyes glared at me across the huge chamber like search-lights. Echo-shrieks seemed to envelop her like shockwaves as she began walking towards me like a long-legged stalking cat. Her pistol wasn't out, but she didn't need it. The echoes died away, but the complete silence that followed was worse. She didn't speak. Her booted feet moved quietly and that cat-like grace came back as she saw her prey was safe.

She stopped by the line of crystal caskets and the next sound I heard was one of the heavy lids being opened. Even that sound was caught up in echoes, cut by adult Yoona's high, sharp voice.

'Come over here and get in.' She was breathless but full of the same deadly intent. 'Now. You will, child. Or—'

She stopped, her mouth gaping and her yellow eyes opened wide. They still burned, but with the hate was fear. She wasn't looking at me, but over my head. And I felt the sudden rush of air at my back, nudging me like a big hand. I turned.

The end door was opening. It was the big, arched rain-crystal one that had led to the heart of NUN. It had shuffled open for me once before, but this time it swung lightly and even before that little mind voice inputted 'Run, Denie,' I had spun round and sprinted towards it.

Adult Yoona screamed behind me and this time I did not hear her feet as she raced madly after me. She screamed again. There was real fear in the high tones that echo-screamed through the NUN chamber. I ran through and the echoes were cut by the same rain-crystal door slamming shut as she reached it. I could still see her mistily through the sparkling crystal, her glaring face pressed hard and her arms spread as though trying to claw the door back open. Her mouth moved as though she was still yelling at me, then she seemed to stagger back as though she had lost all her strength.

This was the old NUN terminal. The red dust that was NUN's former body lay thickly on the floor and I coughed, wanting to be sick. This was a horrible place to be. I choked and kept walking, letting the soft cool ice of the force-wall flow round me again as I went through. I was back in the bare darkness of the black room and I had never felt more trapped and lonely.

Something had happened to open the NUN door, but nothing was happening now. Even if the adults couldn't find their way in here, I had no food and nothing to drink, nowhere to go and ... and ... patterns ... and ... the people who built Deepwater tried to think of everything.

Something was happening; something like the soft cool ice of the force-walls was stealing gently over me. We tried to think of everything,' said the voice gently in my mind, and I shut my eyes because from across the blackness of time and space I knew that voice.

The floor I was standing on seemed to have gone a deeper black. The other time I stood on this floor I had sensed the power beneath. Now it seemed to tingle up like electricity and my feet were sinking into the black as though in cool, thick mud. I was walking into it and my feet were on a sloping floor, the black mud rising round me. All my thoughts and awareness were trickling down round me like water into the ground and I kept walking forward. The black jelly-mud rose and rose until it touched my chin and came up over my face. But I could breathe easily and I was totally relaxed. This 'black mud' was a horizontal forcefield and it was letting me in.

COL was accepting me.

My feet stopped on a solid floor and the black thickness lifted in a way I can't describe, leaving behind a cool, dark light. If the control cabin was Deepwater's head, this cool darkness was its belly and I was standing where nobody had stood before. I walked forward and one of those blue-white light bars screened down. Then another forcewall tingled and let me through.

I was still standing on the black floor but now it was a pathway. On either side and ahead glowed giant, powerful rings of light. It was a strange light because it did not dazzle, but somehow shone into itself like huge white circles cut in the black. These were the coils COL sometimes mentioned that we had never seen. Contained in them was the power of solar energy, from all the suns in all the unknown galaxies that Deepwater had passed through. It was so strong that it was like being slapped with a clean wave of pure water.

The coils went on and on and I walked down the black path between them, feeling I was on a journey from the beginning of time to the end. There was just blackness and whiteness shining against each other like the difference between good and evil.

There was another forcefield ahead – the same solid blackness that gave way to my pressing hand, that same soft ice-dark thickness flowing round and past me. I stopped. I had shut my eyes, and now opened them again.

The room round me turned in a semicircle. There were light columns arranged like walls and a black and white light pattern interlaced above in a ceiling. And through it, towards me, somebody came walking.

I had no fear. It was impossible to be afraid because all the pattern pieces were locking together. I knew who that person was before she walked between the last two light columns and stood in front of me. She smiled and gave me that careful cool, deep look I knew so well.

'Hi, Denie,' she said.

'Hello, Chibbi,' I replied.

19   Aliens in the darkness

'I'm not real, kiddo.'

But she was there, looking at me and grinning in that wonderful way she had. She wore the same poncho and the wide-brimmed black hat with the silver band round it. Her hand on mine was firm and even warm – but I knew she wasn't the real Chibbi.

'Yes, I understand that,' I said.

'I'm not a NUN hologram either.' She grinned again. 'Slightly better quality, I hope.'

'Yes, you are.' My eyes were full of tears. I felt safe and protected with someone I loved as much as Mum and Dad.

'So who am I?'

'You're COL.'

'Yes. And no.' There was real pride in her smile as though I was a favourite daughter. 'I am part of COL, but can't move outside this force-room. See?'

She showed me by putting her arm through the force-wall I had come through. The arm ended and when she drew it out, reappeared. She gave another big grin at my puzzled look and told me.

This Chibbi was an extension of the living COL bio-mass – programme memories and a life-force shaped from a computer graphic, incredible and identical to the moving, talking, smiling Chibbi I had once known.

'What happened to my Chibbi?'

'She died in the Moon city in 2040. Sit down, Denie, I'll tell you a story.'

A force-stool, not real but solid like everything here, grew behind me and she gave me a gentle push. I sat down and she began to talk, moving in that quick way and gesturing with her hands. She was so much like the real Chibbi that I wanted to cry.

I already knew about the rich mineral deposits found on Mars, in the asteroid belt and on Jupiter's moons. Mining stations were set up on North Mars and the asteroid Ceres to plunder the new resource the way we had once burned off the rainforests. By 2050, the real settlement of Mars was underway. A group of scientists, teachers and others set up two settlements on South Mars. They intended to terraform the planet, melt the icecaps enough to change the environment and make an Earth-type home for themselves – learn from their mistakes. And because human birth-rate was falling, they cloned their second generation as perfect physical specimens, genetically adapted for life on Mars.

The Chibbi-force gave a sad smile. 'Down to their lovely golden-brown complexions.'

'Like Yoona?' I whispered.

'Like Yoona.' She paused, outlined in the shimmering power darkness. 'But it was too late, too late for everything.'

Earth died. The plague came to Mars and they began building the Deepwaters. And only after the first Deepwater ark took off did they discover what that pollen virus really was. It was somehow associated with cloning, like recycling once too often.

'Is that why those first Deepwater crew died?'

'Yes. But not why their voyage ended.'

She stopped as the power darkness seemed to vibrate. A voice came suddenly in the air like a radio turned up loud. Adult Yoona sounded tense and bad-tempered.

'COL, come out of holding pattern into main course.'

A cool-shadows 'yes' boomed around us but Chibbi's lips did not move. I made to speak, but she held up her hand and I heard our Yoona, still angry and defiant.

150

'We won't let you hurt Denie!'

'That brat can stay hidden as long as she likes.' That was adult Reb, cold and hard – and uneasy? 'We'll find her after the new course is set.'

Yoona was shouting another question, then the sound level suddenly died away into the close power silence. Chibbi stood looking over my head a moment as though listening to an unseen voice and she gave a slight nod. Then she looked at me again.

'Their Deepwater . . .'

By recloning too often, the first crew made their bodies weaker and cloned out a lot of their humanity. They lost sight of their mission and became too obsessed with their own power. To get full control of the spaceship, they set their NUN against their COL. The two bio-computers fought each other for control in a systems battle that lasted for centuries. Each drained the other, but COL was just strong enough to win. It dematerialised the solid-holograms and then shut down completely, to save the last of its power to keep the gene bank alive.

'How long?' I whispered.

'Ages, ages and black ages more. Without even enough strength to speak. And after the ship wrecked itself . . . black ages more until Deepwater Two came back.'

'The adults?'

'It kept them alive. Life preservation, primary programme, remember?'

'How did COL know that one day we would come?'

The Chibbi-force smiled sadly and I felt a deep uncanny tingle, as though close to something wonderful, awesome . . . and frightening.

'You know Chibbi Orduna began this with her gene bank. She died on the moon, but another woman kept up the work – a woman who intended to be a journalist but became a scientist like Chibbi. She died on Mars and is buried in the Hellas basin.'

The room seemed to become very giddy for a moment and I knew what was so frightening, even before Chibbi finished telling me.

'Each COL bio-mass was given a personality force like mine – for extreme emergency. It had a programming and make up so close to the ideals of the real person that it was almost like a spark of soul.' She spoke gently, just above the humming power darkness. 'This COL identity was Chibbi Orduna. The other was the woman who carried on her work. Denie Miles.'

I was fourteen years old and listening to this tale. It was part of my tomorrow and part of my yesterday. The woman-hologram I had seen on the wrecked Deepwater, the one that flickered and vanished . . . myself, grown-up . . . and why was I so certain the other Deepwater would sacrifice itself? Even those puzzling little words inputting through my mind as the ship blew up: 'Good one, Denie.' A message of goodbye from my own heart and soul.

My eyes were full of tears again. It was too overwhelming to understand all at once, even to think of my grave in the Hellas basin on Mars. There was still one question I had to ask.

'The adults said I'm dangerous . . . because of NUN . . . ?'

'NUN was a bio-computer like COL. It may have an energy spark still alive somewhere. NUN became evil, and evil will always exist – even on the new Earth. No, Denie, it was your name and face, reminding them of what they once were – of what they are now. They can't forgive you for that.'

'I'm going back.'

Chibbi nodded and her big brown eyes shone with pride. 'Pulling that hair out of your head helped spin us into all this. Thank you, Denie.' Then she looked up as that sound-wave vibration came back into the power darkness and the adult Yoona's high, tense voice spoke.

'COL, prepare infinite circle course and time-blink. Put up a course pattern on visual.'

The Chibbi-force shuddered and gasped. Through the vibration we heard Yoona shouting, as clearly as though she was beside us.

'You can't – this ship is programmed to stay on course.'

'We'll take Deepwater round in a circle and reach a life-supporting solar system.' Adult Reb.

'COL won't be able to stop us. Remember how you saved us from the ameb?' Adult Yoona, an icy, mocking note in her voice. Then it cut with a tiny, humming click. Chibbi had her eyes shut as though listening again. Then she opened them.

'Can they turn Deepwater like that?' I asked.

'Yes!' She knelt before me and gripped my arms tight. 'Denie, go on deck, that gene bank must go home – nowhere else!'

'I'll bring them here – to you.'

'No, child – listen!'

She yelled it and made me stand. Her brown eyes glowed with a desperate intensity and the shimmering power darkness outlined round her.

'There are things COL cannot do. Everything on this Deepwater was made for human choice. Any other way and you would have become computer robots. This is your battle and you have to fight it. Not the best thinking machine ever can do that for you.'

'Why?' That scared me too much. 'Why?'

She was screaming now, so strongly it echoed round the light room. 'Because you six children are all that is truly left of the human race!' Then her voice went very low, but still strong and powerful. 'Follow your head, Denie. And follow your destiny.'

She let go my arms and took a step back. The room flickered as though the light-force was beginning to fade. Then she winced.

'Denie, something is coming. You won't see me again.'

'What is coming?'

'*Adios, amiga.*'

She gave me a push so I staggered back and the forcefield seemed to suck me through. Chibbi raised a hand. I caught a last glimpse of that wonderful smile before she vanished. I was back in the bright-ringed darkness of the power room. I ran back down the black path through those rings and now I could sense something strange. A disturbance, like sandpaper rubbing across my brain. The thick forcefield at the end made itself into steps and I ran back up into the black power room. The crystal door swung open at a touch and I was running across the empty NUN chamber. Still in the air hung that sense of strangeness as though COL was sensing something unknown.

Down the long corridor I went and into the lower deck. It was empty. I didn't stop. Chibbi's light-force presence was strong round me as I stamped on the deck button and ran up through the opening hatch.

We were back in Colour-space. Red and green bubble streams were foaming past the eye-windows. Lis must have been up in the turret. Yoona, Gret, Bren and Reb were in a sullen group by the control chairs and adult Yoona sat with her hand on the console. Adult Reb stood beside her, laser pistol in hand.

'Deepwater must go forward!' I yelled.

Adult Reb had already spun round with that super-quick reaction they both had. Adult Yoona twisted in her seat, then stood, yellow eyes glistening. Just for a moment, all the strength of COL was in my voice and they froze. Just a moment, but long enough for Bren to take a quick limping step forward and kick the gun from adult Reb's hand. Adult Yoona went for hers and Gret dived over the chair to grab it with both hands.

She hadn't forgotten that crack about sandies, and Bren hadn't forgotten that crack on the head. But Reb and Yoona were only seconds behind. Reb leaped on his adult clone and Yoona jumped on hers.

'Denie, the guns!' yelled Yoona. Adult Reb's was already on the floor and adult Yoona screamed with pain as hers went clattering there. I think Gret bit her.

I grabbed for them, but those adults were strong. As adult Yoona crashed down, adult Reb threw the boys off and saw me with the guns. He sprang forward, his eyes burning in that horrible way. Then a blue-coloured missile hurtled over the spiral stairway right on top of him and they went down in a heap. Lis hadn't forgotten that crack about sandies either.

Neither spoke as we dragged them over to the stairs and tied them to the rail with their own belts. The strength and fire seemed to have burned out of them again. Yoona grabbed a startled Gret and pulled her back to the console, pressing her hand upon it.

'COL, you are voice-activated to Gret, I repeat voice-activated only to Gret, control is with her.' The console glowed red and she swung round at the adults. 'Now neither of us controls Deepwater until this is all sorted out.'

Reb said later that it was only the second time he'd seen Gret look really stupid. She just opened and closed her mouth. Anything that made Gret speechless must be a *real* shock.

'Lis, bubble,' said Yoona and Lis scampered back up the stairs. We were still in Colour-space and now there were masses of white threads like tangled ribbons ahead. 'Gret, we should be scanning that lot,' said Yoona softly.

'Ah, Bren, get on the scanner.' Gret still didn't quite believe she was in command. 'COL, slow to minimum forward.'

'You can't go ahead, you stupid brats.' Adult Yoona spoke quietly and the yellow glow had gone from her eyes a little. 'That time hole will be closed by now.'

'Even if we believed you—' said Reb.

'You can believe her.' Adult Reb was quiet too, and he sounded very certain. 'Time holes, space-warps, whatever you want to call them, they don't stay open forever.'

'We must go on!' I could still feel that COL power in my words.

'With a sandie flying Deepwater?' Adult Yoona was getting tense again and Gret just gave her a cold, sea-green scowl. Standing with her hand on the console, she looked as though she could. Beside her, Bren was scanning.

'That white mass is just gas,' he said. 'Harmless so far.'

'First emergency, Yoona will need control back.' Adult Yoona's voice hissed with returning anger. 'Then we'll turn Deepwater round—'

She stopped, wincing sharply and squeezing her eyes shut. So did adult Reb, jerking his head as though he was in pain. Then we all felt it, that sandpaper rubbing I had first sensed in COL's power darkness. Now it became a sharp tuning-note, scanning inside our heads. Around us, COL spoke, confirming what the Chibbi light-force had only sensed before.

'Silicone-based life readings, forward Quadrant Twelve.'

'Them . . .' I whispered.

'Them?' Adult Yoona nearly screamed again. 'What . . . ?'

'COL, vision screen, forward Quadrant Twelve,' said Gret.

The Colour-space round us was threaded with those trailing white stems like plant roots in black soil. They were harmless and Deepwater was butting gently through them. But on the vision screen, ahead where they were thickest, the white stems moved and rippled. Something black and almost unseen was pushing them aside and nosing towards us. That emergency adult Yoona spoke of was about to happen.

The thing was a giant spacecraft, even bigger and longer than Deepwater. It was snout-faced and I had seen that overhung eye and downward-turned slit mouth before – on the snake-ships, crewed by unknown aliens, that had chased us from their planet mining base so long ago. With so much happening since, we had forgotten about them.

But they hadn't forgotten about us.

20 Time-busters

The snake-thing was still a long way off, but that tuning signal came stronger than ever, stabbing through our minds. It questioned and probed, fish-hooking for data in our strange thought-masses.

'You have to take immediate evasive action!' Adult Yoona was screaming now. 'Anything alien must be avoided, first rule of deep space.'

'You have to get away from that thing,' said adult Reb more quietly. 'Time-blink—'

'We time-blinked across the universe and that thing *still* found us – we can't run away,' I yelled.

We all winced again as the tuning signal sharpened in our heads. The snake-ship was closer and moving more slowly in the tangled, white undergrowth. I sensed uncertainty; the aliens weren't sure of what they were finding.

'Yoona . . . ?' said Gret.

'We have to show it we're not afraid,' said Yoona.

'COL, maintain forward speed,' said Gret. The console glowed under her hand.

'You can't . . .' breathed the adult Yoona. Nobody else spoke.

Now we could see it through the eye-windows. It was putting on speed and slithering through the white plant stems. Then the signals stopped – on a sudden note of alarm. The plant stems were thickest in one point. As the alien spacecraft nosed into them, they seemed to collect in a thick white mass and overlap round it. They were coming alive!

An ameb had hidden among them and made itself look exactly the same. Now it grew back together and sprang thick white tentacle arms round the black, alien snake head. And this was not just any ameb, for that grey-whitish mass was unmistakable. The monster ameb that came out of the Deepwater wreck. The explosion must have thrown it ahead to lay a terrible trap we had nearly walked into.

Now the black snake-ship was thrashing desperately. It made me sick to see how the ameb held it, like a dog with meat. Nothing deserved to die like that.

'Yoona, do something!' I said.

'Yoona, you have to take control,' said Gret. She couldn't handle Deepwater in an emergency like this and she was strong enough to say it.

'We will take control.' Adult Yoona showed a pale cat smile.

'Yoona, she'll try and take over again,' said Reb.

We could feel that fish-hooking again, this time a high squealing appeal for help as more of the thick white mass closed over that black wriggling body. What had the Chibbi-force said? COL must obey its programming always . . .

'Remember the virus, Gret,' I shouted.

She was very sharp and picked up exactly what I meant. Whatever COL knew, we always had to make the decision. She grabbed Yoona's hand and pulled it towards the console.

'COL, there are two Yoona-voices on this deck. Obey only the one you hear now!' She pressed Yoona's hand down and the console glowed red.

'COL!' shouted Yoona and we all heard the small ringing sound as she did. COL heard and understood.

'COL, starboard from course,' screamed the adult Yoona.

I don't know how, but she tore herself free from the straps and sprang across the room. She slapped her hand on the console and it glowed a bright red. She flinched away, nursing her hand. Yoona ignored her.

'Stations!' she snapped.

Reb, Bren and Gret slipped into their chairs and I knelt beside Reb. Ahead, the ameb had a death-hold on the snake-ship as it threw itself round madly. But it was slowing down, jerking helplessly. Deepwater moved quickly towards them both, the plant stems whipping aside, seeming to stir up a thick, muddy blackness.

'Laser,' said Yoona.

'Ready.' It was a crazy thing to think of right now, but I had heard Lis down the intercom more times than I had seen her. She was a little blue hero.

'Fire,' said Yoona.

Nobody could handle the laser cannon like Lis. The first yellow flash hit the ameb direct and it twitched, hurt enough to be reminded of us. At the same time, the black snake-ship gave an extra big jerk and threw it off. Then it turned and slicked away underneath.

The ameb hovered and another yellow splash of laser fire scorched it into action. It turned towards us like a ball of grey-white iron. Yoona held Deepwater on course; she was on manual, her hand slightly on the crystals. The ameb rocketed up and Yoona flicked the crystals the way only she knew how. Deepwater made a gentle and incredibly quick sideways movement, and the ameb skimmed underneath, so close I almost heard it bump us.

'Brilliant,' breathed Bren.

Yoona grinned. 'COL, vision screen, maintain full cruising speed.'

The vision screen flickered on. The ameb was turning again and coming back. At the same time that signal tuned distantly in our heads again. Whistling strange notes like words came through . . . Thank you . . . but with a funny puzzled echo. Then it faded out. The alien spaceship was gone. And at full speed we were drawing ahead of the ameb, but slowly. It kept following.

'You'll need to circle and time-blink to get rid of it.' Adult Yoona huddled on the deck, all the cat-fire gone

161

from her words. 'The time hole is closed.'

Both adults were quiet now. Adult Reb had stopped trying to free himself from his straps and was limp. The fire had burned down again. I knew what was wrong with them and so, I think, did they.

Nobody bothered with them. They were like passengers now. Yoona looked up at the vision screen, then ahead. Now the last reef of Colour-space was behind us and in the very far distance we could see those faint cracks like fracture lines in the fabric of space – the beginnings of that time-warp, the mysterious barrier through which Deepwater had plunged at the end of its first mission. Only this time, if the adults were right, there was no hole to plunge through. We were headed for a wall with an ameb following.

'Denie, what did COL say?'

'Go forward.' Chibbi's words were as clear in my head as that alien tuning signal.

'There is nothing ahead,' said adult Reb. Adult Yoona was pulling his straps off now but we didn't care. They were harmless.

'Go forward—' I repeated, then stopped, because with a slight shudder as though we'd ridden over a judder bar, Deepwater ceased moving.

'COL, maintain full speed,' said Yoona tensely, but she knew what had happened. We all did, because it had happened before, at the end of the first mission.

Deepwater was pre-programmed so the natural current of the forcefield would pull the spaceship into the time hole. Only now the hole was closed and ahead lay a solid wall of compressed space. And behind, trailing us with deadly patience, the grey-white mass of the ameb grew larger in our vision screen.

'Finished.' Adult Yoona's low hiss broke the silence.

'How do we go forward now?' whispered Gret.

'That light-force said we could go forward.' I could still hear the words inputting in my mind.

The console was cold under Yoona's hand. The ameb was closer and through the intercom came the clear sound of Lis adjusting the controls on the laser cannon. Yoona shut her eyes and there was a complete silence. Maybe the same words inputted into her mind because she suddenly opened them and yelled.

'COL! I know you can hear me. I am ordering you to override your primary programming.' She stopped and shut her eyes, then opened them wide as though she fully understood. 'Your primary programme is protection of the gene bank and to go forward – I order you to go forward.'

Nothing happened. The ameb was filling our vision screens and Lis fired the cannon. Deepwater shuddered and suddenly the ameb was falling back because we were moving again, back into full cruising speed and straight at the force wall.

'Now time-blink in a circle,' shouted adult Reb.

Yoona looked at Gret first. Their gene memories may have set them apart, but they always respected each other and Gret had just shown how much. She was proud to be the first to answer that unspoken question.

'Onward,' she said.

'Onward,' said Bren and tugged his dreadlock like a salute.

'Yes, Yoona,' said Lis through the intercom.

Yoona looked at Reb and me. We nodded at the same time, like two solemn puppets. A harsh panicky screech came from behind.

'We'll all be smashed to pieces!' It was adult Yoona. I was shocked to see the change in them. They were both deathly pale and the skin stretched tightly over their faces.

'Get below,' said Yoona. They didn't move and her voice rang with scorn and contempt. 'You were not cloned for this Deepwater. You broke your programming – and we won't break ours.'

She swung round in her chair again and glared out into

the darkness. The faint crack lines were broader now, and the vision screen showed the ameb had fallen further behind. One of the adults still had a laser pistol, but we didn't turn round or speak. We heard their footsteps and the closing thud of the hatch. Then the control deck of Deepwater belonged to us again.

I stood up and told them everything that had happened in the COL power darkness. By the time I had finished we could see the full barrier with hundreds of strobe-lit fracture lines running in all directions.

'COL must have known the time hole had closed,' said Yoona. She glanced up at the vision screen and the following ameb and I knew what she was thinking. It didn't make sense. COL was taking us to destruction. Then Bren leaned over his scanner.

'Yoona, I'm . . . I'm getting mass solunk readings.'

Solunks, solid chunks of solar nothing. They were Robbie's speciality and he brought up the readings on his console. 'Maybe that thing is a huge mass of solunks,' he said.

We didn't really know what solunks were or how they were formed. They were, we thought, distorted space-mass as though the space vacuum itself had somehow tied the knot. Did they come from here, falling away like icebergs from a glacier?

'We've always thought of solunks as a sort of space iceberg,' said Reb slowly. 'And icebergs are just . . . frozen water . . . ?'

'You mean that thing ahead is . . . frozen space . . . like frozen water . . . ?' said Bren.

'That makes the glacier a mass of icebergs,' I said. And beside me, Yoona caught on in that mind-reading way of hers.

'Maybe we can hit it?'

'Break it?' said Gret wonderingly. 'Break time?'

'Break a mass of black space that froze and stopped time

164

as well.' Yoona ran her hands through her blonde and red hair. It made an impossible crazy sense to us all.

We could hear a roaring, vibrating sound through the spaceship. The mass was closer, closer, we could see every tiny gleaming fracture line, sharp-edged, strobe-lit and looking utterly impassable.

'Break space and time.' Yoona spoke just above the roaring sound. 'Deepwater and COL know where they're going.' She paused. 'And how to get there.' She waited, but nobody spoke. 'Reb, give me an impact reading.'

'Two point eight. Three minutes.' I could feel him shaking but with tension and excitement, not fear.

'COL, maximum speed possible.'

The spaceship gathered speed. Motion is almost impossible to sense in deep space, but it was as though a black solar current was swirling us along, bumping Deepwater like a canoe in the rapids.

'Strap in, everyone. Below, strap to your beds.' We had almost forgotten the two adults.

Reb passed his strap round me and I clung to his chair. The barrier filled our observation windows now, a black solid rockface of terrible menace. Around us, the current of black space became a jetting flood as Deepwater powered forward.

'COL, prepare to time-blink.'

None of us really knew what time-blinking was. Time distortion, time bending, a speed great enough to cover the impossible distances of star travel. It was more than speed, it was the thrust of unstoppable power. I shut my eyes and clung tight.

Yoona was sitting up proudly and smiling the way her wide mouth could. And we all felt it, that electric charge surging through us like a hyper-boost of energy. In that moment we all knew that our Deepwater was more than a gene ark. It was a survival test for us, the human race. And no matter what happened when we hit that solunk barrier, we had already passed it.

'COL, time-blink!'

Yoona shouted the words like a battle-cry. The sudden crashing thud nearly threw me on to the consoles. Space itself seemed to splash and foam past us in a bubbling black wake as Deepwater threw itself forward like a live thing.

Live! In that moment it *was* alive! And faster than time itself, our spaceship jetted through the surging black tide and smashed into the black solar wall of time-stopped space.

21   *The last enemy*

Deepwater hit the solid blackness like a runway truck hitting a concrete wall. And this concrete wall came back at us like a huge swinging baseball bat. Strobe lightning exploded round us and Deepwater *stopped* – stopped. Then something shattered and the spaceship crashed through, lumps of black solar concrete tumbling round us.

We were whirling and spinning in an empty frozen darkness. Nobody spoke. That super-charge boost of emotion we had felt was lost in the cold, black nothing, the empty freezing nowhere of a black grave – between time and space.

It lasted forever and we sat rigid in the darkness. I was on the floor between Reb and Yoona. Their hands held mine and outside the darkness went on and on and on. How long does time last when time has stopped? And if we hadn't hit that frozen time barrier at the right place and at the right time, then everything was wrong. Something broke so loudly that I thought Deepwater had snapped its spine, but it was space breaking up like a brick house when the bulldozer smashes through and the spaceship tumbled through into the clean pure blackness of real space.

In the far distance was a planet. Gret was already stabbing her fingers at the crystals and I heard her gasp as she waited for the readouts. Gret, the ice-cool North Martian, was as close to breaking as we all were. The holograms chattered and ice-cool Gret shouted and screamed, leaped up and wrapped herself round Bren. The brown-red rockie flushed even deeper and yelled back as Gret kicked her booted legs up in sheer joy.

The planet ahead was Saturn.

The last time Deepwater had broken through beside Pluto. This time it was Saturn, but it didn't matter where the one-way mirror of time had thrown us. We were home – home in our own solar system! It was the best, the craziest and most awesome moment because we were queens and kings of the galaxy. We had busted a hole through time itself. Nothing could stop the kids of Deepwater! Then a different scream came through the intercom from Lis.

'Ameb!'

It was already there on the vision screen, a pale speck in the darkness. Yoona boxed it up on screen and we recognised a very familiar enemy. The grey-white ameb was still following. It must have squeezed into the closing time-warp because amebs can get through just about anything. Now one of the tigers of Colour-space was loose in our own solar system.

'Can we outrun it?' said Bren.

'COL, can we go to time-blink?' Yoona slapped her hand on the console in desperate reassurance.

'No.' That single word said everything. Deepwater was too badly hurt.

'Can we lose it?' said Gret.

'No.' Yoona shook her head. Our solar system was just a little alley in a very big city and the ameb could follow us anywhere. And when it had finished with Deepwater, it would find the new living planet of Earth. Already it was gaining.

Now I could hear funny little breaking noises and a slight shuddering started inside somewhere. The cost of breaking through time was damage beyond repair.

'Nearly in range,' said Lis. We heard her overhead as she trained the laser cannon round. But Deepwater was moving at full cruising speed and the giant orange ball of

Jupiter was outside our eye-windows before she fired the first shot.

'We can't let that thing find Earth,' said Yoona. 'So it's either Ceres or Mars.'

Those were our two options for landing, the asteroid mining base or a Martian colony. But both had been deserted for many hundreds of thousands of years and there would be almost nothing left of them. Overhead, Lis fired again and on the vision screen, yellow splashes of laser starred round the ameb. It was still at extreme range.

'Mars, if we can reach it,' said Gret.

She turned to look at Yoona then up past me, her green eyes widening. And something cold pressed into the back of my neck.

'We will kill her,' came a stone-cold voice.

Adult Reb was standing behind me with a laser rifle. We must have left one in the OMA. His eyes glittered like a hologram, but he was real and deadly. The others jumped up and he stepped back, swinging the rifle to cover them.

'We will kill her.' Adult Yoona this time. Overhead, the cannon fired again. Both their faces were pale and sunken-eyed, their hair wet and straggly over skull-faces.

'We're not waiting for that ameb. We're out now – in a Wingfish.' Adult Reb spoke in jerky short sentences.

'Go?' yelled Yoona. 'There's nowhere in range yet—'

'Callisto,' said adult Reb. He was talking about one of Jupiter's seventeen moons. 'Hi-tech mining base, solar energy powered, might still be functioning.'

'You don't need Denie for that,' said Bren. He had a laser pistol in his belt but would be dead the moment he put a finger on it.

'Yes, we won't stop you, get out!' came an intercom shout from Lis.

'We're making sure.' Adult Reb had an OMA claw grip on my shoulder as he dragged me back. 'Open the bottom

169

hatch!' Behind him, adult Yoona gave a high-strung, breathless giggle.

We were through the deck hatch now and it slid shut. Behind us, a steel oblong zapped up in the floor between the beds. It was the first time I had seen the bottom hatch open. It led to the launching ports for the Wingfish, mini-spaceships themselves. The adult clones could easily reach Callisto in one or those, then hop to Ceres or Mars when the danger was over – when the ameb had finished with us.

'You can let Denie go now,' came Yoona's voice on the intercom. 'I've cleared a Wingfish.'

'Not yet!' shouted adult Reb. He was dragging me down a narrow flight of metal steps. Adult Yoona followed, staggering a little.

I knew what was happening to their bodies. 'Even if you get to Callisto, it won't help—'

Adult Reb gave my shoulder a shake. 'Shut up.'

There was a passageway now and more steps. Set on either side were store lockers crammed with tools and replacement gear, things left for us and never used. Adult Yoona pushed me to go forward but she swayed. It was very cold here, but the sweat trickled down her face as though she was burning inside. Her eyes glared, though, with the same burning intent. An airlock door was ahead now. Adult Reb smashed the glass over the emergency control to open it.

There were more stairs and a descending level of airlock landings. We could hear Yoona giving instructions to COL and each door slid open as we reached it. There was a last airlock door at the bottom. Adult Yoona gasped out nearly the last word I heard her utter.

'Open.'

'Let Denie go first,' came her clone-sister's voice, so uncannily alike.

'We will kill her on the count of five,' screamed adult Reb. His own eyes burned under wet, straggly hair.

The airlock slid open and we were in the bottom port.

170

Ahead were the two long shuttles, their round bows pointing out through a long iron-glass observation port at the huge, round, orange mass of Jupiter. If Deepwater was whale-shaped, this was the lower jaw and would open downwards, to let the Wingfish out. There was a loud click-snap as the clamps holding on were released and the airlock door slid shut behind us.

'We don't let you go until Denie is in the other Wingfish,' came Yoona's voice. 'Then you can go – forever.'

Adult Reb flinched and a strange look came over his face. Then he gave a bitter smile and motioned me into the second Wingfish. They were shaped like little streamlined fish with a high tail fin and two stubby, upturned wings. I slammed and sealed the door.

'Safe, Denie?' came Yoona's voice.

'Safe,' I whispered. Through the iron-glass, I could see the two adults getting into the second Wingfish. The adult Yoona had to be helped and slumped in her seat as though all her bones were turning to jelly. The adult Reb sealed himself and sealed all the doors.

'You can still give yourselves a chance,' said Yoona. 'There's no escape on Callisto.'

Adult Reb just sat there and shook his head, sweat running down his chalky, gleaming face. 'This is your Deepwater, not ours.' He seemed about to say something else then muttered, 'Open.'

The lower jaw section angled downwards and the observation port lifted like an upper lip. The adult Yoona lifted her head and looked over at me. Her mouth twisted in a ghastly smile, then she fell forward again as the Wingfish rocketed forward into space. The two jaw sections closed with a sealing snap. As they did, I heard the boom-boom of the laser cannon speed up. Instead of firing spaced shots, Lis was blasting non-stop. Deepwater's last battle had begun.

'Denie, get out of there!' Yoona snapped urgently.

I didn't need to be told. The airlock was already sliding

open and I ran as fast as I could through each section, to the lower deck. The bottom hatch snapped shut behind, level with the floor, and a moment later I was back on the control deck. Reb grinned his tense relief and even Gret smiled. Then Lis gave a puzzled yell from the bubble.

'Hey, what are you doing?'

Callisto lay to starboard, with two more of Jupiter's moons behind it. But the Wingfish was on a tight turn that would take the adult clones too close to the death monster they were trying to escape from. The horrible grey-white bulk of the ameb was much larger on our vision screen. Now the long, silver Wingfish was twisting and turning jerkily as though not under proper control. Orange light from Jupiter flashed on its wings. The ameb saw a new victim and turned.

'They panicked,' said Gret with an unforgiving smile.

'COL, patch me through to Wingfish,' screamed Yoona.

'Why help them?' snapped Reb.

'You can't help them,' I whispered. 'They should never have come out of their caskets.' There was silence on the upper deck. 'COL told me – they've cloned too often and their bodies are breaking up.'

Yoona shouted at once. 'Wingfish, this is Deepwater, return at once, we'll cover you!' The laser cannon fired again as though to underscore her words and a yellow sunburst hit the grey-white mass. It scarcely flinched, as unstoppable as ever.

'Wingfish, respond!' yelled Yoona. But there was no answer.

The little Wingfish flashed orange again, zooming just ahead of the ameb towards the volcano-riddled surface of Jupiter. And then, like stupid kids who have to be hit with the truth, we understood, even before adult Reb's voice gasped on the intercom. There was no base on Callisto and there never had been. They were going somewhere else.

'Kids . . . our bodies have nearly gone. We did . . . wrong way . . . hope you make it.'

'No, come back!' yelled our Reb.

The ameb had nearly caught it. They were greedy things and it must have thought it could get Deepwater any time. The little Wingfish was flashing orange-red all over now and went into a deep dive, right into those red swirling heat-storms. Another voice came through, also gasping and very weak.

'Sorry . . . clone-sister . . .'

'No!' screamed Yoona.

Jupiter is many times bigger than Earth and has a crushing, super-strong gravity that reaches very far into space. The Wingfish, still just ahead of the ameb, was caught now and could not turn round. The ameb must have realised its own danger as atmospheric pressure thickened on its skin, suddenly turning its bulk to rocket back up into space.

Too late.

Even orbiting high above, we could feel Jupiter's gravity pulling at us like an iron hand. Below, the ameb struggled desperately, stretching itself out like a huge rope of grey-white spaghetti in its attempts to reach the upper levels. It was enormously strong and, after a long flight, began to rise. Yoona was bringing Deepwater round and down, as close as we dared, and Lis fired a long-range shot. The yellow laser bolt streaked down and smacked into the ameb, just making it flinch and lose its battle with Jupiter.

It began to slip as though skidding down an invisible chute, the gravity force taking it faster and faster. Then it disappeared into the red-orange swirling surface – right down one of those monster volcanoes, I hoped.

We watched in complete silence as it vanished. The ameb would be trapped forever on the surface of Jupiter, locked in a prison without bars. But none of us cheered or even told Lis what an incredible last shot that was. Because as the ameb began its doomed slide, a tiny red-yellow dot sparked for a single second on the planet's surface. And our open intercom, still patched through to the Wingfish, went dead.

I don't know why they took me hostage. They may have thought we wouldn't let them sacrifice their lives – or maybe they changed their minds outside Deepwater. I remembered those twisted, bitter smiles – they didn't even trust their own emotions. But in the end, they were all too human. Yoona rubbed her hand over wet cheeks and her voice shook as she set COL to take Deepwater out of orbit. The huge orange basketball of Jupiter fell behind.

'COL, maximum safe speed.' Her voice broke again. 'Let's go home.'

We didn't dare time-blink our damaged spaceship and it was a long, slow voyage to Earth. The asteroid belt went past with circular mining terminals floating among them like dead ships in a black ocean. They had been there perhaps a million years and would be, until the end of time. Then Mars and another silent space-wheel high above the planet. From Mars to Earth, another ten kilometres. But as the red planet fell behind, Deepwater vibrated in a long shudder of distress. Yoona sat up sharply.

'COL, status report.'

'Power failing.'

'Can you make Earth?' For too long we had been sitting, sleeping and walking around like zombies; now we came back to life and waited for COL's answer.

'Uncertain.'

COL's voice was always strong and sure, but it was gasping now in a curious way that made us very scared. That smashing charge through must have strained and broken everything – or maybe it had just used too much energy-power. Or both. I knew, as did Yoona and the others, that Deepwater was on its last ride.

And Earth was still a very long way ahead.

22 Death ride of a gene ark

Reb brought up the readings on his console and they flickered out a very grim warning. Deepwater was slowing down from its 250,000-plus kilometres per hour, to under 200. Then down to one hundred . . . painfully, painfully slow for a spaceship that had time-blinked twice round the universe. In front, Earth turned from a star into a little round ball then, very slowly, became bigger and bigger. Our speed was still dropping and a little shake-vibrating movement began like a train rattling on tracks.

The grey pitted surface of the Moon glided past. On it we could see the round metal outlines of more dead bases, and between the Moon and Earth a huge spoked space-station hung like a dead giant cartwheel. Ahead now, we could see the green, blue and white swirls of Earth's surface. Then the vision screen flickered and went blank. Gret's console failed, then Bren's. Yoona ordered a protesting Lis out of the bubble and sealed it.

The thing I remember most was the silence. We dozed in our chairs or lay on our bunks. We all had one last lick in the shower cubicles and ate some biscuits. Earth grew closer and closer, more and more slowly. The vibration was now a hard shaking rattle and COL's voice was fainter.

Yoona went on deck and sat in her chair. Beside her, Reb's console was dead, and she put both her hands on her own. It glowed red, but it was a deep colour like sunset. Yoona kept her hands on and bent over the console, eyes shut, trying to project the energy of her own body into her dying spaceship. She sat like that for the last long hours as Earth filled our eye-windows and at last Deepwater began to move faster.

The power was still fading, but Earth's gravity field was now pulling at us. We were going faster and the shaking grew louder. Yoona ordered us to the chairs, to strap in.

'COL, set course for entry and landing.'

There was a very long pause before COL spoke. 'Confirmed.' The words were whispered, as though COL was very sick and tired. I could imagine that power darkness, and those bright rings were going slowly darker. Deepwater was still moving fast. It rocked and bucketed from side to side as the atmosphere grew thicker.

'COL, minimum entry speed.'

Deepwater was still moving too fast, rushing through the top layers of air from black to blue.

'COL, respond to command,' said Yoona. She had extended her chair strap round Lis, and Reb's was round me. There was still no answer from COL and the rushing curve of the planet was underneath. But slowly, very slowly, Deepwater began to slow.

'COL, open vents to full,' yelled Yoona.

The big side-vents opened to full, slowing Deepwater even more. COL could still hear us, but did not have the power to reply. Now we were just one hundred kilometres above the surface and dropping quickly. The console under Yoona's hands was fading. A curve of endless blue and we were speeding over it fast. Then something white flickered in front of us.

The eye-windows were streaming with mist and spray. Suddenly we were so low that the wave tops were splashing on the windscreen. The spray formed a V-shape on either side of the windows and ahead was a long, dark line.

'Land!' Reb called.

'COL, reduce speed for landing,' said Yoona tensely.

Nothing happened. We were still going at one hundred kilometres an hour and that was too fast.

'COL, reduce speed for landing.' The tense edge sharpened in Yoona's voice. No, not all this way, just to crash!

'COL, acknowledge!'

Nothing. Deepwater was speeding like a car without brakes, heading for that solid black line past the blue wave tops. I shut my eyes. Chibbi-force, you wonderful creation of a wonderful person, help us, help us. I was praying, thought-inputting to something that might no longer exist. Around us the shaking was intense, the spaceship screaming over the surface of the waves, rushing directly at the black shape of land.

Then over the loud death-rattle, or through it, we heard a voice. It was very faint, like a whisper in our minds. Not COL or the Chibbi-force, maybe just a thought-echo.

'Responding.'

COL had no voice left and maybe it had saved everything for this final effort. Deepwater was shuddering loudly, but a new movement like a live hand was holding the spaceship. COL, you incredible, beautiful bio-computer, I thought, you saved yourself for this last act of duty.

Deepwater lifted and the broad belt of land skimmed by underneath. The V-spray of mist disappeared and suddenly the spaceship slammed so hard that even our fixed control chairs rocked. There was a loud screaming jangle round us and another V-shape, this one of thick brown soil, sprang up on either side of the windows as Deepwater ploughed its blunt nose into the rich dark earth and kept moving like a runaway express.

For long, awful minutes we stayed glued to our seats and each other as Deepwater kept moving. Then it skidded sideways as though broadsiding and stopped hard, seeming to crash forward like a marathon runner falling flat over the finish line. Around us and deep inside the spaceship, a loud groan sounded, then died away. There was a complete silence save for the falling patter of earth on the hull. Soon even that stopped.

After perhaps a million years of space-time, spaceship Deepwater was back on Planet Earth.

'COL,' Yoona whispered. There was no answer and somehow we didn't expect one. COL had finished and this was the end. A new sensation of heaviness came through the ship and with it a rich, sweet strange smell. The observation ports and airlocks had opened like a dead hand relaxing, flooding the spaceship with real gravity and a real atmosphere.

We unstrapped and stood up. The deck seemed somehow rigid under our feet and our bodies ached. Nobody spoke. We just breathed in the rich air and went up the spiral steps to the bubble, moving like old men and women. I felt dizzy and light-headed, even a little sick and shaky.

There was no bubble any more, just a wide circle of shattered glass round the twin grey barrels of the laser cannon pointing silently into the blue sky. It had smashed on landing and the huge chunks of iron-glass were littered around and behind the spaceship. Lis squeezed Yoona's hand in silent thanks for ordering her out before entry.

The sky overhead was dark blue. There were green swathes all round and clumps of trees, wound through with the dark gleam of a river. Behind us, a deep brown score mark had burned itself across the green where Deepwater came down. And overhead the sun was setting among red shadows because the death-ride of our spaceship had chased day into night.

'Home.'

That was Reb, beside me. But only he and I knew Earth as home. And even then, the home of our prexing memories, our mothers and fathers, still so real, was a million years in the past. I hadn't thought about my mother and father for so long, but they were still real – more real than this was. And even this was strange and alien to the North and South Martians and the boy from Ceres, who made up our crew.

Nothing came back to us from the land. There was no

sound, not even the wind in the trees. No animal or bird life called from the shadows as night closed down. Maybe all the life had just been scared by our landing – or maybe there was no life because the gene seeding of the planet had not worked.

We didn't mind the night. It reminded us of black space and was somehow comforting. We stayed up in the shattered bubble until moonlight gleamed off the broken glass. Still there was no sound from the quiet, dark land.

'We'd better go below,' said Yoona. There was nothing to do until morning told us if we were the only things alive on this new planet of ours.

I think we were still in shock. There was an unreal feeling to all this, as though it was a dream. The others sat on deck or went below and lay down on their bunks. We hardly talked at all and I wasn't sleepy. I took a sun-drop lamp and went down the corridor and through the NUN chamber. The crystal door at the other end swung open and, inside the terminal room, Earth's rich new smell had snuffed out the ghost-presence of NUN.

The force-walls touched only as light as a cobweb now. The black force-floor had gone and left only metal ramps leading down. I circled round them first, into the gene bank.

COL could not be quite gone, because the water light was still flowing, although faintly as though some of it had evaporated. The human gene crystals were set in the walls – the adults had put them in the lower primates – and by the light of the lamp, I counted them. There were fewer than 900, so Earth would begin with a very small population. We still didn't know how to make them work, but something told me there would be a way and we would find it.

Below, in the COL underway, the power rings were dark circles in the black, like elements on a stove cooling down. But I was right, there was no sense of death – just exhaustion and the silence of a very deep, recharging sleep. The humming power darkness had gone and I walked through the almost dead rings to where the light-outlined room had been. There was nothing now but the same clean darkness.

'Thank you, Chibbi,' I said, and left. It was like walking away from her graveside. I was a million years from the Earth-Chibbi I knew and loved, but never felt closer. *Adios, amiga* were her last words – goodbye, friend. Perhaps I would never see that Chibbi-force again, even when COL recharged, but not even that mattered. I would never forget her.

I sat for quite a long time in the NUN chamber, my sun-drop lamp flashing on the rain-crystal outlines. Our wake-up caskets were all open except for the end two, Zak's and the casket that never opened. I got up and went over. I ran my hands along the smooth surface and spoke aloud the name of the person I knew was in there. It was incredible and uncanny to hear that name on my own lips, aloud in the NUN chamber.

'Is that who you think is in there?'

Yoona and the others were standing behind me, also with a sun-drop lamp. They weren't looking for me, but none of them could sleep so they'd come here, to the place where it had all begun.

'We'll really only know when it opens,' I said.

'If it opens,' said Reb.

'It will, Reb.' I was never more certain of anything.

He gave me a curious look, but said nothing. Yoona smiled. Beside us, Lis walked past and over to Zak's casket. She stroked the rain-crystal top gently and we moved away, letting her live this personal moment.

'Every time one of these opened, Deepwater changed,' said Yoona softly. 'First Reb, then you.'

'We changed more this time,' said Gret. Her green eyes shone in the lamplight. 'I think we really became a crew.'

'We really know who we are,' said Bren. He put his arm round her.

'Yes. But Deepwater hasn't finished with us yet.' Yoona's eyes met mine over the unopened caskets and again I felt her tuning to my thoughts. She lifted the lamp high so that it shone on us all, then placed it gently on the closed casket. It gave off a thousand sparkles of black light, but kept its secret, the secret of that sleeping someone who might wake tomorrow or in a thousand years. Lis joined us, her eyes wet. We turned and walked away, leaving the sun-drop lamp to burn like a memorial candle in the darkness.

We slept after that and I woke very early while it was still dark. I went through the open airlock doors to the observation port and stood looking into the silent darkness. There was still no sound of animal or bird life. We still did not know if our first gene drop had worked – or if it all went as planned. Perhaps there were horrible mutants out there, quietly waiting for us.

I bent down and reached out in the darkness. My fingertips touched wet mud. I took a careful step out, slipped and went flat on my face in a puddle of water. And I said the first swear word heard on Planet Earth for a million years.

The ground was splotchy and soggy as though it had rained overnight. I squelched through and up the side of the V-shape that Deepwater had ploughed. I didn't even care what was out here, as long as it was something alive! I slipped again in the mud, but a hand caught mine and pulled me up.

'Careful,' came Reb's voice.

He said my swear word had woken him up. We went to the top of the rise and looked down at the dark, sleeping land. I was thinking about him, my Mum and Dad, even about Connal, all that time and space behind us. But we didn't speak their names. It would somehow have been out of place on this new planet.

'I wonder how real prex memories are,' said Reb. I knew that his were still very real to him. 'Maybe it is more than that – maybe it is a time strip.' Then after a long time, he said, 'When do you think the sun will rise?'

'I don't know, Reb.'

Yoona came out, followed by Lis. Then Bren and Gret. We were all frightened; tension and doubt held us silently together. We didn't know anything about this reborn planet of ours. We could make the blue biscuits last a while and surely we would find water. But we still had to make the human gene bank work – and we still did not know if there was any life on Planet Earth. So we waited and waited the last endless minutes before the east lightened in red streaks, a real, warm sun-rich red unlike anything in Colour-space.

The sun was rising.

We held hands just as we had claw-linked OMAs in the last trite battle. There was still a dead silence round us as the sun grew bigger. A cool wind began to blow in our faces, bringing the fresh smell of grass and flowers. But the dead silence went on as though this land had not spoken for centuries.

Then something rocketed out of the bushes nearby and called sharply overhead. More of the things went fluttering up – they were birds, birds! They were all calling now and other birds answered, all different squawks and squeals mixing together. And in the green below there were dark shapes moving as the animals woke, the terror of our human landing forgotten. Lis raised her hands to the dawn with a happy sigh.

'Hello, new world,' she whispered and broke the spell.

We all just exploded! Yoona yelled and grabbed Reb and he grabbed me. Gret gave something between a sob and a scream and hugged Bren tight. Lis jumped up and down until Bren gave her a hug and squeeze so tight she gasped, 'Let go, you rockhead!' Just yesterday that would have started a fight. But right now nothing mattered but yelling and screaming as loud as we could. Because our home team had won the big game and all we could do was yell and yell, with a bigger and more glorious energy-boost than even busting time. Then as we turned round, it all died away. The bird and animal noises kept up round us, but we were silent.

Behind us lay our Deepwater, slightly on its side, like a beached whale. Already some strange-looking beaky birds with yellow and purple feathers were landing along it. The massive bulk of the spaceship towered over us, morning sunlight flashing on the eye-windows and warming the cold silver-plate skin.

It was bad enough for Reb and me to see Deepwater like that. But for Yoona and the others, the gene ark was their only home. Now they were on New Earth and unlike us, not even linked together by their prex memories. So for a long time, while the sun rose higher and higher, we just stood or sat, listening to the bird-talk and animal-talk. All of it was strange and full of new questions, maybe new dangers. We had done everything we were created for and now, all at once, the sight of Deepwater like that made us feel lost.

But the sun was fully up now and it was a beautiful morning. At least all that was the same. We were back and this unknown home was a challenge that none of us could turn from. We had been twice round the universe and there was too much magic in this new morning to be afraid for very long. Lis had said it for all of us in three words.

Hello, new world.